"I look at every single man to see if he looks at me. I can see at once if his eyes are alert and gleaming. I notice at once whether he is a man, whether he is contemptible or all right, whether he has courage or is afraid, and I secretly desire — I secretly desire every single man who understands my femininity."

I, A WOMAN

I, A WOMAN

by

SIV HOLM

Translated from the Danish
by J. W. Brown

A SEYMOUR LAWRENCE BOOK
AN ORIGINAL DELL BOOK

PART ONE

On the outskirts of town is a two-storied yellow-brick house. It stands facing the sea with its back to a small, pleasant wood. In front of the house is a tidy garden with sharply defined flowerbeds and narrow gravel paths, the whole fenced in by a low, closely clipped hedge.

A wide gravel road runs from the end of the house to a courtyard containing neat piles of scaffolding and lumber, a chickenyard and a chickenhouse. Behind lies a large, luxuriant and well-kept orchard and garden with fruit trees and vegetable beds, and, beyond, a velvety lawn which by no means must ever be walked upon.

If a complete stranger comes to visit the yellow house, he walks through the white garden gate, through the front garden and up to the front door, which is always locked. If, however, he has been there before, he walks up the wide gravel road, across the courtyard to the kitchen door, which is never locked, and he enters a warm, friendly kitchen, the heart of the house, from which doors and hallways lead to the other rooms.

It is night, a warm, light spring night. But although it is three o'clock, there are lights on in all the rooms, a fire in the stove and boiling water in the pots. Because it is during this one night, at this particular time of year, when the gods, intoxicated with love, dance and empty their seed over the heavy expectant earth, that a child is born in the yellow house.

The father wanders restlessly about in hastily buttoned trousers which have been pulled on over his white night shirt. His wiry black hair hangs, like a disordered mop, over his thin tanned face. A lock of hair has wandered desperately down over his drawn eyebrows, and the deep-set eyes have a curiously stern and flashing expression.

His nose is large and coarse, and deep wrinkles encircle his mouth and chin. A vigorous mustache half covers his tightly closed lips. His jawbones jut out and his skin is so taut that his ears follow the movement of his jaws. His head as a whole is small, his body lean and slender. This man seems to be all face, face and eyes. A strong, ugly, masculine face, a face which challenges life itself to battle.

Where does this Bushman come from?

From a gypsy wagon—from the poorhouse.

A woman died, a child stood beside the wagon. No one knew who the father was, and the boy landed in the poorhouse.

When he was nine years old he began to work for the farmers. He slept in filthy rooms and was covered with fleas and lice; the boys and girls slept together in the same beds of hay. He grew up slowly on a diet of bread with grease and potatoes. But he grew up, and his thirst for knowledge and learning was unquenchable.

His fantastic self-discipline helped him; he worked and wandered, saved and learned.

He is now forty-five years old, a master carpenter, and has picked up knowledge about mathematics, languages and many other things.

But what good is a man when he walks around in his own house with his hands, usually so busy, clenched nervously in his pants pockets, when the whole house is full of women and his beloved wife lies stretched out on their broad double bed and, with fearful groans, prepares to give birth to his child, their first after fifteen years of marriage?

No, he is no good at all. He is absolutely nothing. He can do nothing more than promise himself that he will never place her in a similar situation again. He feels forsaken and unreasonably betrayed, excluded as he is from the woman's world.

After all, he is only a man.

A scream is heard from the bedroom. He walks into the other end of the house, bites his pipe stem in pieces, is raging mad with everything and everyone, but mostly with himself—and he is terribly frightened.

Once in a while he becomes humble and prays to his God.

A woman comes through the door. He stands up, tensing his jaws until they stand out like hard knots beneath his brown skin.

"Well?"

"It's a girl!"

He chews on his damaged pipe and half turns away. "Hm—yes!" He then turns again toward the woman and asks threateningly, "How's my wife getting along?"

"Splendidly. She wants to see you."

"Now?"

The woman smiles patronizingly, taking him by the arm. "There, now. Come. It's all over."

He staggers out of the door like a drunken man. He stops abruptly in front of the door to the holy of holies and opens it with extreme caution, stops at the foot of the bed and looks at his wife with a gruff, embarrassed expression on his face. "Well, little Ino?"

The mother is thirty-seven years old, red-haired. She whines contentedly.

She has light blue-green eyes and a gentle, chubby body. Her smile is gentle, as are her voice and her gait. She is the exception that proves the rule that redheads are full of temperament, violent in love and hate, warmhearted, charitable and capricious.

She is Finnish, with broad Mongolian traits, and seems, in spite of her femininity, somewhat coarse and vulgar.

But now she only lies there in bed, happy, exhausted and proud.

"Come here, Sacho."

He walks over and sits down on the edge of the bed, bends over her, trembling, and carefully kisses the pale, soft face. "Are you all right?"

"Yes, but it hurt so, Sacho."

"Hmm."

"Don't you want to see our child?"

His eyes follow her lifted hand; he gets up and carefully approaches the curious thing the midwife holds between her hands, a wet, slimy thing that shrieks as if it wants to inform the whole world of the unhappy event that has just happened.

Because the mutation is born. Half gypsy, half Finnish. A long-haired, black-haired, purple girl who screams the mistake all over the house.

Sacho shakes his head in surprise and smiles. "What an ugly creature. Have I really had anything to do with making you?"

He is stopped by Ino's reproachful voice. "But, Sacho, isn't she wonderful? Aren't you happy to have her?"

He turns and looks teasingly at his wife. "Sure. She's the eighth wonder of the world."

He then walks into the parlor, sits at his desk and takes out his Bible, folds his hands upon the book and thanks God fervently because things turned out so well.

Yes, he is a Christian, a fanatic, uncontrollably lost in worship of the great Christian God with all His rules and promises. He fears his passions, his secret desires, having damned them to eternal destruction on behalf of this Christ with the crucified hands and the crown of self-denial on his brow.

He believes in heaven and hell, God and the devil, and good and evil with a cuttingly sharp line drawn right through his own mind.

And he never goes to sleep in the evenings until he has forced his soul to rest in the fatherly hands of God.

CHAPTER ONE

Fourteen years have passed.

An autumn full of rain and storm. The last blood-red leaves fall from the vine which grows, thick and luxuriant, up toward the eaves of the house. The dark, cold sea washes the coast. An icy fog from the sea surrounds the house and its garden.

A young girl walks down the street. She has on a raincoat and a rain hat which envelops her pale, thin face. Her skinny legs rush urgently toward the yellow house.

There is a serious, thoughtful, perhaps preoccupied expression in her dark, burning eyes.

This is Siv Esruth, the girl, the fourteen-year-old mutation, who, every time she nears the yellow house, approaches it almost like a stranger, feels herself to be a stranger. It is quite true that she crosses the yard and opens the kitchen door, smiles and says "Hello" as if she were at home. It is quite true that she is the daughter of the house, a very spoiled and loved child.

And yet. Every time she nears the yellow exterior with its shiny windows, inhales its warmth, its cleanliness and its quiet, pleasant atmosphere, she has to fight her way through her own mind, blink her eyes a little and force herself to remember that it is here, precisely here, that she belongs.

But once she has entered the kitchen and has answered the familiar questions from the familiar voices, once she has sat down upon the bench by the window, smiling her girlish smile, only then does she return. Even then she might have to shake her head to get rid of her strange, preoccupied mood, shaking her thoughts into words and smiles, becoming warm and attentive.

It is only because she is a bit queer once in a while when she takes walks all by herself.

11

But it is depressing for her to meet her mother in the kitchen today, because her father is lying sick in the big, bright bedroom with its reddish cedar bed. It has something to do with an infection and the clotting of his blood, which can be fatal.

Do the grownups really think that her father can die?

It cannot be true.

One day her father had shown her a piece of oak, brownish-black, stone-hard and indestructible.

That is what her father is like—a dark, tempered piece of oak which cannot decay.

Over her parents' bed hangs a piece of cloth framed in glass. Embroidered upon the cloth in large letters are the words "Behold, behold, I am coming soon!"

Siv understands it in this way: her father will live until Christ returns to the earth.

But it is quiet in the house, cold in the parlor. There is an emptiness by her father's desk. It is warm only in the kitchen.

Siv sits down upon the woodbox. She looks at her mother. She just wishes that there was some other place in the house that was warm—because she can hardly stand it here. Her mother's soft plump body seems to be dissolved by tears. From her slippers to her red hair, which is beginning to turn gray with a yellow cast, there radiates a pitiable air of complete resignation. Disgust creeps through her whenever her mother looks at her. She can never keep her sorrow within her; it always has to seep out all over her body.

Siv nervously kicks her feet. *You* have to conceal it, at any rate, you have to try to; it is best that you hide it, isn't it? She begins to feel knots of malicious stubbornness inside her.

Her mother turns. "Ugh," Siv thinks, "now she is going to come over to me," and she sits as stiff as a stick when she feels the soft arms around her throat, a wet, flabby cheek against her own.

"My little Siv, Mother is so unhappy. We have to be nice to each other, we two."

Siv carefully frees herself, runs her eyes over her mother's face—and smiles. That was the worst thing she could have done.

"Siv!" Her mother's voice is sick with reproach. "Are you laughing?"

"No—it's not because I'm not sorry about Father, it's just that your face suddenly looked so strange."

"Strange?" Her mother becomes an *abyss* of bitter, uncomprehensive reproach.

"Yes, in a way, it looks as if it's been half-wiped out by an eraser."

Her mother quietly walks over to the bench by the kitchen table, hides her face in her large, white apron and sobs quietly.

Siv sits silent and tense. She cannot go over to her mother and say that she is sorry. She wants to die of shame.

Her mother raises her head and looks searchingly at her. Siv stands up. She has to get out of here. So she starts to walk slowly toward the door which leads to the garden. She stops abruptly. "It doesn't help Father when we cry like this. I cannot stand any more." And she works herself up to the point at which tears fill her eyes, so that her mother can see that *she*, too, is unhappy.

A glimpse of hope enters her mother's eyes. Is Siv crying?

She stretches out her hand, but Siv hurriedly opens the door, yanks her coat off the hook and walks down to the sea.

A few hours later she is standing by her father's bed. The bed is placed beside the window, and the cold, sharp daylight shines on the white sheets and on the huge pillow which sticks out in two points above the thin, brown face. He has not been shaved for two days and looks very sick.

Siv looks at his hands lying on the blanket. They are thin and bony, with thick, expanded veins. Good, hard hands—father's hands, strong and worn.

He looks at her from beneath his bushy eyebrows, twitches his mustache, smiles. "So there you are, my little girl."

"Yes." Siv nods and smiles—with a large lump in her throat, because she suddenly is struck by the thought that her father is a little child, and this is a completely absurd thought when she herself is fourteen years old.

"You don't have to stay here, dear."

"Yes, Mother wants me to sit here until she comes back—but you're supposed to sleep."

Her father has already closed his eyes, his breath comes quickly and with difficulty, and there is no peace in his face.

She sits quietly with her hands in her lap, observing him.

She could kiss *him.* But she has never been allowed to do that. Well, a quick kiss on his cheek after he swings her into the air, a hurried embrace around his stomach, with her hand clamped tightly and securely in his. But never a warm, lingering caress. She believes her father is embarrassed by caresses, at any rate from her. It is different with her mother, but, then, she is his wife.

Her father has "sensations" when he holds her mother, the same sensations Siv feels when she fights with older boys or reads a forbidden book.

Does her mother have the same sensations as well? She probably does—once in a while. But it is impossible for Siv to imagine it.

Her father, on the other hand! She has seen his face when he has touched her mother's breasts. Also, one night when she sneaked downstairs to get a piece of bread, she heard something through the half-open door of their bedroom. She heard her mother's voice whining, "Oh, not again, Sacho. I'm too tired!"

And then her father's growl, "I've *got* to, Ino."

She had been angry with her mother. If there was something her father wanted to do, shouldn't he be allowed to do it? Why wouldn't her mother let him?

Father, dear, why do you love Mother?

Siv knows about such things. She has seen the dogs in the street with their tongues hanging out of their mouths and their excited eyes as they jump upon each other. She knows all about it because her father explained it to her. She *had* to find out, and you don't ask Mother about such things; that would have been too painful and humiliating.

But her father had explained it all calmly and objectively. "Like cats and dogs, Siv, human beings are also a kind of animal with that same difference below—but because we are *human beings,* we are not to act like animals. We're supposed to be faithful to a particular person, the one we love and marry. Otherwise we sin. That's God's law and we do best to follow it." He had looked very earnestly and seriously at her. "Remember, Siv, remember this when you grow up, because God has arranged it so that what you do to get a child is a pleasure, and therefore it can be very difficult to hold back, to wait until you're married."

Her father told Siv all this, and much, much more. He explained the pure anatomical differences and conditions to her.

And she understood that what he had explained to her was very serious and difficult, because her father usually did not use so many words.

And now she sits there beside his bed with a flood of affection, clinging to the thought that her father cannot die!

But what if it should happen just the same? She knows very well that everyone has to die some day; then her father will go to heaven. "Father, you're a Christian, and you really want to go to heaven. It won't be difficult for you, you know that, don't you?"

Siv has been given very many new things to think about; many new things have taken place within her body and mind.

It is evening a few days later. Her father is still very sick.

Siv is sitting in the kitchen doing her homework at the table. It is too cold in her own room up in the attic.

The door to the bedroom is half-open. Her mother is in there with a lady from the Missionary Society.

Her father is feverish and nervous. Siv strains to hear what he is mumbling.

"It's strange to think that you're going to be put into the ground."

Ino's voice: "But, Sacho, you're going to get well."

The strange lady: "And even if you don't? You know that you belong to God, don't you?"

Father: "Yes, I really want to believe that I belong to God."

Siv drops her pencil, sits completely still, her heart beating strongly, empty with fear: Father's not sure? Oh, how awful.

Her father mutters: "I've smoked, you know."

Her mother: "Smoked? But, Sacho, the minister also smokes; I don't think that *that's* a sin."

Her father: "I've often felt myself damned because of it. It's not right to let something get so much power over you that you can't control it."

Siv does not want to hear any more. She packs her books together and goes up to her room without saying good night.

To think that God can be so hard on my father!

She does not say her prayers that evening.

But her father gets well again—and he does not smoke any more.

He seems smaller to Siv. Imagine, to be *that* afraid of God.

Strange people begin to visit their home. Her father goes to a different place for prayer meeting. New magazines and pamphlets come, too.

Her mother looks dispirited and reproachful, but her tears are of no avail. Her father wants to attend these new meetings. He wants to read these magazines which contain so many new things that he has never thought of before. This new sect believes in the Bible as it was written for the first apostles. They believe in the baptism of the Holy Ghost, adult baptism, healing through the laying on of hands and the paying of tithes to the congregation's treasury.

Many new friends come to Siv's home. They call each other by their first names, because they are brothers and sisters in the Lord—and they are happy.

Some bring musical instruments along: mandolins, violins, lutes and—ah! the harmonica.

They play and sing.

Not hymns, at least not like those Siv has been accustomed to hear. They are happy dance tunes, light and rhythmical. The text is about God, but it is quite different from the text of traditional hymns:

On Sunday I'm so happy,
On Monday full of joy,
On Tuesday heaven nears me.

Oh, what a song of joy!
On Wednesday and on Thursday
I feel so very fine.
On Friday and on Saturday
What bliss, what bliss is mine!
Oh, glory, glory, glory. Oh, glory to God's Lamb.
I am free and I am saved: I have my love in Him.

They stand gathered into a flock in the front parlor, with
its red covers on the sofa and armchairs, with all the fragile
glass trinkets and knickknacks, where everything is so
clean. They fill the room with warmth and song, tapping
their feet, keeping time, and are joyously full of God.

Siv thinks: Can my father really sing such songs? But
her father just sits on the sofa, folds his hands and looks
kind, watching them.

She thinks about her father's violin, which hangs on the
wall of the room where his desk is. It hangs there beside
the newspaper rack and the brown telephone. It has been
a long time since her father has played it, long before
his illness.

He usually played it when he was angry, nervous, sad or
moody. It had a terrible, delightful, shuddering, lamenting sound—a good sound.

But now it just hangs there gathering dust, because her
father, calmly and quietly, folds his hands, and a violin
is of no use to folded hands.

Siv wanders around the house. Things spin around inside her when she stands in front of her father's violin:
What if she took it in to them? Her father could then
play it with the others, couldn't he?

No, no. He could never do that. That would be terrible.

They sing again in the room of glass.

She walks back to the half-open door and listens. It is
a song about blood!

His blood, His blood is a mighty flood.
Wash yourself clean in the Lamb's dear blood.
His blood, His blood is a cleansing flood.

Many of their songs are about blood. Siv thinks that they
wallow in blood. She becomes sick at the thought of all
that blood.

And what about their old church? What about all their old friends from the Missionary Society?

Aren't they going to get into heaven?
Which place would God rather be?
Where is He now?

CHAPTER TWO

A few months later both her father and mother joined the new congregation.

They wore long, white gowns and let themselves be ducked under the water in a large pool. The music played, people cried "Halleluja!" because two more people had been led into the path of righteousness.

Siv had sat down in the hall and watched. At first she had been a little embarrassed, but she too was soon captivated by the atmosphere. She had also been somewhat upset, because she wasn't "saved."

She felt absolutely sure about that. You cannot be saved when you go around the way she does, with sinful thoughts on your mind and strange sensations in your body. But, so what! Life is long, and she will surely manage to be saved some day before she dies.

And she has been given permission to cut her hair!

Her thick, wiry, black hair had been braided into two taut, stiff ropes of hair throughout her childhood. She looked upon this as her martyrdom, because she knew very well that braids did not suit her. Her face is little and narrow, her nose a bit too large, her mouth as well, and the tightly drawn hair gave her face an old expression. She had been an ugly child, little and thin with long skinny arms and legs, but with gracious, expressive movements and burning, brown eyes.

But now she has been given permission to cut her hair, and it seems to have brightened her whole being.

It happened one evening when her father and mother had been to a prayer meeting and afterwards were sitting drinking coffee in the kitchen.

Siv had not gone to the meeting. She had to do her homework. Afterwards, she had read a book which she had borrowed from one of her girl friends. It was called

The Sheik's Favorite Wife, and was a book which she was sure her father would not approve, so she had hidden it carefully among her schoolbooks.

She had sat reading until her eyes and ears burned.

It was all about a beautiful English lady who had been captured by a sensitive, terrible, but heavenly desert sheik.

He wanted to—she would not—oh, the whole thing had been so very splendid.

She had changed the ending because it was not any good as it stood. The sheik lets himself be tamed by the beautiful English lady, but Siv imagined that things turned out the other way around.

She had sat at her desk up in her room, biting her eraser, had crossed her legs and played the English lady.

Afterwards, she had gone down to the kitchen to join her father and mother. She had looked at her father with flaming cheeks and shiny eyes and asked if she could not be allowed to cut her hair.

"Oh, Father, I look so ugly with these braids—and I'll soon be fifteen years old. Can't I cut my hair a little bit so that it just hangs loose?"

At first her father had not noticed her. He had been far off in his own thoughts. He sat there talking to her mother about the strange things they had experienced. Her mother had been baptized in the Holy Ghost and "spoke in tongues" at evening prayer. Her father could not manage it, but looked enviously and admiringly at her mother.

Finally her father had noticed Siv, slowly nodded his head, pushing his Bible across the table and nodded again. "Why, yes, my dear, of course you can."

Both Siv and her mother were surprised that everything had gone so easily. You could never really understand what was going on inside of Father. Perhaps he hadn't really thought over what he said, filled as he was with God and the Holy Ghost.

And yet, he had looked so affectionately at her, smiled a little, as if he understood the reason for her request just the same.

And so now she has cut her hair. She ties a ribbon above her forehead, shakes her hair so that it brushes against her cheeks, and jumps for joy in front of her mirror. "Now I'm no longer ugly."

She runs down into the parlor and turns around in front of her father and mother. "Look!"

Her father nods with pleasure, her mother with worry. Sacho's God makes him worry.

"Sacho, your daughter is beginning to grow up, haven't you noticed? She has small, pointed breasts and her narrow hips are supple and swinging. Sacho, what are you going to do? How are you going to protect this girl against life? You want her to be saved, but look at her. Look at her: a long-legged, delicate girl with sex flashing in every nerve, with the dark eyes of a slave and fluttering hair so good to take hold of. Sacho, you have no idea what a mistake it was for your faith when you sowed your seed in your wife and begat this creature."

But Sacho's God sits in his mind, not in his blood.

He looks at Siv with a man's eyes, like a proud father —and grunts contentedly.

Siv becomes very popular at school.

The time is past when she had to stand in a corner watching the other girls walking arm in arm with each other, whispering and giggling.

For Siv there seems to be no middle ground. Either she is hated or she is loved and admired.

The boys nudge each other and mumble, "Have you seen Siv? Look how she's changed!"

The girls hear this—and see it.

One of them comes over and takes her by the arm. "Come, don't you want to walk with us?" Siv is dizzy with joy, her loneliness is over.

The girls show her their "kiss-books." Any girl with an ounce of self-respect has her "kiss-book," in which the number of kisses she has received are carefully written down, who kissed her and when.

Siv thinks it nothing except a lot of foolishness, but she does not say so. Everything is so nice now, and they are all so sweet. She had never noticed it before.

But the oldest boys at school are only sixteen years old. Sixteen years old? They have piping voices, are full of swaggering, embarrassed eagerness; their eyes are mocking but unsure.

Siv feels serious uneasiness only when she is confronted

by a grown-up man, but she keeps this a deep secret. It is so wonderful that the girls no longer think she is "odd."

But what if she is kissed some day by the right man? What will it be like? An experience that cannot be described?

She writes love poems for the girls.

Everybody knows that it is Siv who writes them, but that doesn't matter. The boys read them, eagerly and ecstatically. They throw stolen glances over the fence that separates the boys' playground from the girls', laugh, wave to their brides-to-be, overlooking the ironic smile Siv gives them as she walks arm in arm with their beloveds.

They are only playing—all of them.

CHAPTER THREE

Siv is at school, in her math class.

She cannot do arithmetic, has never been able to do it, and never will. Nothing helps, neither the best math teacher, the most energetic teacher, nor her own desperate efforts.

Her face is turned toward the blackboard. She looks at the numbers: something about the water capacity of a half-filled well. Completely incomprehensible!

First, there is the fact that you *have* to study it, then the fact that you have to be able to do it.

It makes absolutely no difference to her whether the well holds a few gallons more or less.

She now looks at her teacher's back instead. His back is broad, his neck is broad, and the chalk disappears in his huge, rough hand.

He turns to the class and explains.

What color are his eyes? Gray? Blue? She must remember to find out.

He has a friendly but determined personality. The girls are a little afraid of him. He boxes ears in the boys' class. That never happens in the girls' class:

But perhaps he *could* be made to do it just the same. Suppose he really got angry?

As Siv sits there she feels a terrible desire to provoke him to see whether he really *would* strike a girl.

"Will you come up and continue, Siv?"

She is startled.

"Will you finish working out the problem on the board?"

She stands up, but stays beside her desk. "I'll go to the board if you like, but I can't do the problem."

"Haven't you been paying attention?"

"No, and even if I had been, it wouldn't have made any difference. I don't *know* how to do math."

Her teacher says sarcastically, "Don't you know any of your multiplication tables?"

No answer.

"What's seven times nine?" Silence. "Won't you answer?"

Siv breathes deeply. Now it is going to happen. "No, and I don't care."

He walks up to her. "You don't care?"

Her playmates hold their breath. It is deathly quiet in the classroom, drama in the air. You can see it in the teacher's insecurity, in Siv's flushed half-mocking face.

"What a shame one is not allowed to give girls a beating."

Siv's voice is husky when she asks, "Why can't you?"

Her teacher is startled—makes a move—is about to strike.

Then she says quickly, "It wouldn't do us any harm, you know."

Their eyes meet. She sees that his are gray.

A blush spreads across the man's face, right down to his powerful neck.

He understands. She really *wants* a beating.

He looks at her, and Siv lowers her head in shame and compassion. Disheartened, she thinks: "Beat me, beat me until I no longer find it so amusing. Do *something!*"

There is a powerful silence between them. Men are good, handsome and polite. That is the way things are supposed to be. It is just that Siv needs something else.

She raises her head and looks beseechingly at him. "Excuse me, I didn't mean it, I—I—"

"Yes, you!" he interrupts her vehemently. "You—you are incredible!"

The class is over. The girls stand in a flock around her. "Why did you say such things to him?"

Siv, embarrassed, shrugs her shoulders. "For the fun of it!"

"Oh, you're crazy!"

But they walk out into the yard in a united flock with Siv among them, and they look at each other with their secret, feminine, nervous thoughts, but do not talk any more about *that*.

When school is over, Siv takes her bookbag and hurries home. She runs as if she had a swarm of bees at her ears, crossing streets and squares, down the wide avenue lined with trees, down the hill and home to the yellow house near the wood and the sea. Home to a large plate of sandwiches and piping-hot cocoa, home to the world of her childhood, where you can be just as impossible and bad as you want to be—and still be loved!

When she comes into the kitchen, breathing hard, and throws her bookbag down, her mother looks reproachfully at her. "But, Siv, what's the rush? You'll soon be too big to act like this. Walk properly so that you don't get out of breath."

Siv looks at her bag and waits for the next sentence which is: "You know very well that I won't have that bag of yours in here. Take it up to your room. Why do I have to tell you the same thing every day?"

Yes, why does she have to? There is no reason in the world.

But it is impossible for Siv to put her bag away at once, just as it is also impossible for her to walk the last blocks home from school so that she does not come in the door out of breath. Yes, it is just as impossible as it would be to get a trainman to drive his train backwards or in the wrong direction.

"Are you going with us to prayer meeting this evening?"

"Yes."

Because then she won't have to go to bed before eleven o'clock, she will be treated like an adult—and her father will be happy.

Her mother nods, content and pleased. She now has two chins under her first. She is round and healthy, but does not seem fat. She is so fragily built that a lot of fat would be needed before she would look unappealing. Her round, soft shape only makes her look even more contented and childishly happy than she did before.

Her father likes her mother to wear bright colors, and that is the reason her clothes are red, green and yellow, festive, harmonious colors. Her hair has become grayer, but it is still soft and wavy, as fine as silk. Her cheeks are flushed with a healthy pink, and her movements are eager and quick.

Sacho is fond of his Ino.

When he comes home in the evenings, she rewards him with a soft, anxious smile. "Are you tired?"

He gathers his strength. "No, not enough to mention!" Or he feels the need for her gentleness. "Yes, a little."

And he is fed his favorite dish and sinks down into this feminine warmth and care.

Just the same, once in a while, deep, deep down in his eyes is a reserved, mocking, condescending look which makes his face look tired and closed.

He has sold himself to his duty, cut himself off from the indecent world of desire.

But he stiffens his slender, brown neck and mixes his daily cocktail, which consists of: a motherly wife, a decent life, child and home—spiced with a fear of the fires of hell.

He swallows his cocktail, bows his head and thanks God.

But he travels in the evenings!

He sits beside his large globe of the world. Thick books of travel stories lie in front of the round sphere. He sits at his desk with his back to the room, mumbling something every now and then, nodding in wonder, enchanted by these unknown things, tightening his jaws because of his pent-up curiosity and his bad conscience.

Siv often sits hiding behind a book looking at her father's back—with a painful compassion in her soul, with an unexplainable bitterness in her mind: Why is she sitting here feeling sorry for her father? He has what he wants, that which he himself has chosen, hasn't he?

But afterwards she looks at her mother's happy, contented face—and becomes angry: Father is beginning to get old; he has never seen any of the places he has dreamed about. But mother! *She's* happy, of course!

This evening, however, they are going to prayer meeting, and Siv would like to go along. Since her father thinks that it is the right thing to do, well then, it *must* be the right thing, though there is so much she does not understand —even in the Bible.

It is written there that Cain traveled to a strange land and married the daughters of the land! How could he do that if his father and mother were the first people on earth?

And what about the Virgin Mary? If she conceived through the Holy Ghost, well then, this spirit had to turn into a man for a while, with everything that a man has below his belt, didn't it?

But you are supposed to believe everything in the Bible, childishly and naïvely. She must control her thoughts; otherwise she will be lost, and she *wants* to be with her father in heaven.

They put on their wraps and walk to the bus which will take them to "The House of God," and Siv is happy and proud because of the flashing glances of affection in her father's eyes.

But deep inside of her there is something which protests: Father . . . ?

They are sitting in the large hall. There are benches along both sides of a wide aisle. There is a speaker's rostrum which reminds her of her teacher's desk at school.

Beside the rostrum is a platform where the choir sits. They play lutes, accompanied by a piano. The music is good, merry fresh and clean, the voices clear with a sensual undertone which captivates Siv.

The choir is composed of young girls with glowing coals in their eyes. There are also older people, but only their cheeks are aglow.

But they sing and play well!

Religious people are musical—and sensual, because God is the father of the senses!

Only these poor, hungry women do not know it!

Neither is Siv completely aware of it, but she feels herself uplifted by the singing, feels a holy eagerness in her soul, an ecstatic enthusiasm: This must be heavenly music.

Now the whole congregation sings together. It is not so beautiful. But everyone tries to sing as well as he can:

> He will fill me 'til I overflow.
> When he calls: "Come to me!
> I shall give my blessing to thee,"
> He will fill me 'til I overflow
> With His Holy Ghost and might.

Afterwards, the congregation stands and the leader begins the prayer.

He begins and a mumbling choir of voices swells up in the hall.

Some stand groaning: "Halleluja!" Others: "Amen!"

Some pray to themselves with many words.

The voices gather into a mumbling whole; excitement rises.

The atmosphere becomes heated, seductive, sensual. Holy ecstasy is released.

A woman begins to "speak in tongues," another translates, and a slow sobbing is heard from the rear of the hall.

Siv is carried away by this atmosphere, she is paralyzed, excited, ecstatic.

This must be God!

CHAPTER FOUR

Siv's breasts grow, her womb bleeds once a month and her thoughts swing back and forth between piety and stimulating fantasies about strong men.

Her time is taken up by evening prayer meetings, school and the whispered exchange of confidences among her friends, by reading the Bible together with her father and mother before going to bed, and, afterwards, reading forbidden books under the covers with a flashlight.

Siv has become quiet and serious, thoughtful and absentminded at home. She remembers only half of the things she is to fetch at the grocery store and goes home knowing that she has not bought the right things.

Her mother chides. Siv nods quietly and says, "All right, all right. I'll go back and exchange it. Yes, I promise I'll remember.

She says yes, she says no, she nods and smiles with a preoccupied air, resigned to things as they are.

She helps her mother in the kitchen, shirks half of her work, is indifferent, quite thoroughly unconcerned. She does not even make an effort to hide her mistakes.

Her mother is tired of railing at her, tired of hammering against the apathetic wall which has risen in Siv's mind against all reasonable, everyday things.

Her mother complains to her father.

"Of course, Siv is to do what you ask her to do."

But he gives her mother the job of straightening her out, giving her a loving pat on the cheek before turning back to his desk.

The teachers at school have also had enough of her. She never prepares her assignments properly. They believe she can do the work, but won't. And they are right.

Why won't she? She doesn't even know herself. She

doesn't even care. Why can't these grown-ups, who want to do her so much good, just leave her alone?

Her German teacher, Miss Litzen, really *wants* Siv to buckle down. She says that Siv has a "gift for language," and that it is a pity, a shame and quite meaningless for her not to learn her grammar.

But Siv does not want to sit cramming in what is feminine, masculine and neuter. What a lot of foolishness to give *things* sex.

She likes history. Her teacher is pleasant, sitting there at her desk with folded hands telling about the wars and great men of past ages, explaining intrigues and terrors in a voice that crackles and shakes with excitement.

Yes, her history class is warm and pleasant.

But, then there are all those dates!

Naturally Siv could manage to learn them, but she won't—won't—won't—she won't do anything in the world that is not exciting. She makes no attempt at all to remember when this or that happened, and she coldly and calmly tosses out a completely idiotic date whenever she is examined.

But she doesn't hate school. She doesn't hate her teachers. She just feels sorry for them. She is just a little tired of them. They mean well. But you can't do anything with people who believe that such things are a matter of life and death.

What is it that really does interest her? She has no idea, but she is constantly expecting something or other, expecting in a tired, gnawing mood which makes her silent and reserved.

But Miss Litzen, her German teacher, is unable to be indifferent. Siv has become her passionate obsession.

One day, she is friendly and talks quietly and intimately with Siv. "Tell me, Siv, why won't you ever do your homework the way you should? You who have such ability and could be so smart. Is there anything bothering you? You don't have to be afraid to tell me, you know."

They are alone in the classroom after her German class. Siv looks at her teacher and discovers that she looks like a horse, a kind, miserable horse with its head on an angle. Bothering me? There is nothing bothering me—and what if there was?

You can never feel completely safe when you confide in grown-ups. It is impossible for them to understand—they really do not *dare* to.

Just think if she told her that the only thing bothering her was the fact that she was not grown-up enough to have a man? Just think, if she told her that.

She looks at her teacher's sad horse-face. She snickers and quickly looks away from those tired eyes with their white circles around the blue irises. Dead, tired eyes. But, then, it must be awful being a teacher, especially when you take your job as seriously as Miss Litzen does.

"Why are you smiling, Siv?"

Her teacher has turned off the friendly expression in her face and now looks strict and accusing.

"Well—because there is nothing bothering me, except perhaps that I'm not old enough to quit school."

"Are you tired of going to school then?"

"Yes," sighs Siv, her face in deep, anxious creases, but she looks at the floor, hiding her eyes so that the sparkling, clear joy always found at the bottom of her pupils won't betray her. Because she is not tired of going to school. She is not tired of anything in the world. She knows that some day she, too, will be an adult and will experience everything.

But she only sighs and looks at the floor.

Her teacher pats her on her shoulders. "You'll see. Everything will turn out all right."

What do very young girls do other than wait and wait? They don't read newspapers. They are not interested in politics. They don't think—they just feel.

These very young women are so new that they have not discovered that the world is about to be transformed, and that the difference is about to be balanced. They still believe in a man's strength, believe it is greater than theirs, that it is their prerogative to be stupid, ignorant and illogical, sensitive women. Later—much later—they discover that they have to be both man and woman. Then they are quite at a loss, become uneasy, domineering and, oh, so logical.

But now they play tennis, take long trips on their bicycles with their friends, they swim, row, ski or ice-skate in the winter. Whatever they do, the only thing which fills their minds is the thought of big boys, young men and mature men.

The world is at war!

Of what concern is it to them?

In the evenings they stand in gateways, snickering and whispering, in pairs, for only then do they feel themselves to be safe.

They still play "cops and robbers" even though they are almost grown. It is delightful to be captured by the boys, to be shaken and pushed by eager, hard hands, to have your arm twisted behind your back so that you have to beg for mercy.

They dress up, they measure how much their breasts have grown. They are hysterical and unpredictable, cry and laugh for no reason whatsoever. And they look in every mirror, every shopwindow to see if their hair is as it should be.

They notice every man they meet, looking out of the corners of their eyes to see whether he notices *them* and whether he looks indifferent or admiring.

They are small erotic demons! They can flirt, or behave like ladies. They can say "Ugh," and "No," and hold fast to their virtue, or they can be short and to the point and willing like Siv. They can admit their longing and search for its gratification or they can flee in genuine fear.

Yet their greatest wish is the same: rape!

Forgive the poor men who sin against these small erotic demons.

Some day they will be able to leave a man's embrace and begin to think philosophically. But before that day comes, you must not expect them to be wise and reasonable. They can only wish, yearn and feel.

Though worried people make other laws, this is the law of nature for women.

CHAPTER FIVE

Siv wakes up on the morning of the ninth of April and discovers that war has come to Denmark.

She goes to school and the principal assembles all the pupils in the gym. He speaks to them in a voice weak with emotion. There is to be no school today; they can go back home, but they are to behave calmly and with dignity: they are not to talk to the strangers who have occupied their country, but neither are they to annoy them. It is going to be a hard time, he said—for everyone.

Siv walks home from school trying to feel the weight of what has just happened. She walks slowly and with dignity, somewhat self-importantly. She puts her feet down hard upon the asphalt. This is *her* country, she must not forget that. That is what her principal had said.

She turns her head and looks at the trees lining the avenue, at the houses, and she can catch glimpses of the woods and the water. Then she raises her head and looks at the sky with its light clouds. There are also houses, trees and streets in Germany. The same skies are above them, and at night they can see the same stars and the same moon.

But the earth? Siv scrapes her feet. The earth here is Danish, it is called Denmark. Does that make any difference? The adults think so.

She has been told the story about the Danish flag, which fell down from the skies. But a flag is only a piece of cloth, used to decorate the town on festive occasions.

Germany also has its piece of cloth, only it is a different color.

She has sung in school "I love my country." She has also sung "Denmark, you small, you wonderful land."

And she likes to sing.

But other countries are beautiful, too, aren't they?

She feels depressed because she does not love her country more than she loves other countries that have forests, fields, blue skies and sea. Because she does not like Danes any more than she would like Germans, Englishmen, Frenchmen, Russians, Americans—yes, any more than she would like all the people in the world if they smiled and were strong.

When she comes home, her mother meets her with eyes red from crying.

Siv bites her lip, but says nothing: Things can't be *that* bad.

And her mother's tears mean nothing.

She has seen her mother cry over the newspaper when she has read about accidents, murder and violence, the starving Chinese and the oppressed Negroes. She has seen her mother cry uncontrollably over some mother's early death which left a lot of children orphans.

But she has never seen her *give away* anything!

Siv remembers the times when her father invited poor people into their kitchen. He talked with them and called them by their first names.

Her mother stood by the stove, her cheeks red with indignation. She whispered to her husband, "What on earth have you done this for? There's not enough food for them, and have you seen their hands? They could at least have washed! And they wouldn't be so poor if they'd force themselves to do a little work."

Her father grumbled and looked at her mother, causing her to be quiet out of fear. They were on bad terms for several days afterwards.

Sacho also gives money to the street musicians who earn their living by walking from house to house playing fiddles, mandolins and harmonicas.

"How much did you give them, Sacho?"

"A crown [fifteen cents]."

"Oh, was that necessary?"

Ino never gives anything away but her tears.

Siv stands at the window in her father's room looking down the street. Long rows of vehicles are driving past. Trucks, tanks, field-kitchens, motorcycles and troop transports.

Her father has come home. He stands there, too, looking out of the window.

Siv has not read the newspapers, but she knows, at any rate, that the war has lasted a long time, that the Germans are fighting against England, America and Russia, that they have occupied Poland and the other small countries that once belonged to Germany, and that they have now occupied Denmark and Norway. She has heard that they persecute and kill the Jews. They have also hunted down gypsies. They want to create a pure Aryan race; they want a place in the sun, to show the world that they are the smartest, the biggest and the strongest.

They must be like Napoleon. He also wanted to overturn the world.

Siv understands *this* much. But she looks at the tired, dusty soldiers marching, driving, yelling and toiling past her house. She looks at their round steel helmets and their gray uniforms—and is surprised!

Because there are *human beings* inside the uniforms.

And she does not hate them.

She wonders what her father thinks about the whole thing. She has looked at him several times. He is silent, standing there with his hands behind his back, just *looking*. Siv does not dare ask him. He looks so austere and seems so far away.

A division of the infantry comes marching past. They sing as they march. Siv shivers with excitement. She looks at her father once more: What is he thinking about *now*, I wonder? She cautiously asks, "They sound good, don't they?"

Her father looks at her quickly, with his sharp, bright glance. The hard features of his mouth soften. "Yes, Siv, it's good to hear young, strong male voices."

He turns back to the window, sighs and lets his clenched fist fall heavily on the windowsill. "But what I can't stand is that they come storming up here as if they owned the place."

The following day Siv goes to school as usual. The streets, the people and the houses look just as they always have. There are planes in the air and scattered groups of German soldiers, but otherwise nothing is happening.

She is unable to feel that there is a war.

They get ration cards, but nobody starves.

They get orders to cover their windows, and the adults fuss around with black curtains, trying to fix their windows so that they can avoid a fine.

But Siv walks through the streets in the evening and finds the darkness exciting.

The adults talk about the war and, my God, how many different points of view they have. Siv gives up trying to figure out who is right or wrong.

One says that it is the law of nature. So many people *have to be* wiped out, either by war or disease, in order to control the human flood.

Another maintains that money is the cause of war— and who has money? The Jews. Therefore the Jews are the cause of war.

A third thinks that the Germans—and only the Germans—are responsible for the war.

And the Christians put all the blame on Satan!

A fourteen-year-old girl is generally quiet, listens, watches—and perhaps has an opinion. But whatever it is, she keeps it to herself. Her mind cannot grasp and understand all the terrible things she hears. She believes that it is everybody's and nobody's fault.

She dresses up and laughs. Because she is young. She only wants to live and be young.

CHAPTER SIX

Siv is in her last year of school!

She comes home with bad grades in mathematics. Sacho shakes his head with disapproval. "This will never do, Siv. You know you're soon to take your final examinations."

She assumes that it is quite impossible for her to understand mathematics. As soon as she has managed to get all the small, stupid numbers into her head, they get muddled up and disappear.

Her father grumbles and says that she must have a private tutor. She *shall* pass her examinations for her diploma; otherwise she will never be able to manage later in life.

Her father speaks to a young student who belongs to "the congregation." He studies at the university and is the pride of the sect.

Siv remembers seeing him at the prayer meetings, but she has never really spoken to him.

He looks very wise and learned when he enters the hall in his impressive red and white student cap. He takes it off, revealing his thick, blonde hair and sits down unpretentiously at the back of the hall. Siv has also seen how he then takes off his eyeglasses and rubs his eyes with his long fingers.

See, how tired he looks from all that reading! She shudders. It must really be awful to have to study for so many years. To sit there thinking about every single sentence, learning it all by heart.

But it is good for a young man to be industrious, they say. It is a sign of good, strong character, proof that he wants to *become* something.

She has also noticed how very polite and helpful he is.

He stands up to give an old lady a cushion, straightens her coat, or helps her find her eyeglasses in her handbag. And he smiles warmly when she thanks him.

"A splendid young man!" whispers the congregation.

Student Svend often has his violin with him. He walks up to the piano, sets the case down, opens it, takes out the violin and rubs the bow. And he does all of this while looking very serious. It is kind of him to want to help with the music.

The women send him friendly and appreciative looks. "It was nice of Svend to come this evening. It's so nice to have a violin accompany us in unison singing."

Siv looks nervously at the door, hoping that Ella, who plays the piano, will come early enough to tune the violin. She always reaches for it without any fuss. It seems quite natural that, when she sits down at the piano, she also tunes the violin.

One evening Ella does not come.

Siv rocks in her chair. He's going to have to tune the violin by himself, and he will never manage! Also, since there is no one to play the piano, the violin will have to support the unison singing.

The meeting is to begin in five minutes. The violin lies on the piano, waiting. Svend sits on the first bench, waiting, confident and happy. He will soon pick up his violin and entertain all these people.

Siv's hands are moist because of her painful knowledge. She nudges her father. "Couldn't you go up and tune Svend's violin?"

Her father smiles. "Of course not. That would hurt his feelings."

"Oh, please." Siv's eyes are desperate and beseeching.

"I'll do no such thing!"

If she only dared do it herself. She moves uneasily.

Her father grabs her sternly by the shoulder. "You stay right here!

Her mother nudges them to make them keep quiet. "Don't be so silly, child. Svend has played the violin ever since he was eight years old. I'm sure that he can tune it himself."

Despairing, Siv looks up at her father. He sits there with a funny, contracted sneer under his mustache.

It is of some comfort to her to know that she is right.

Either you can play or you can't. What good is it for him
to stand up there with his long, thin violinist's fingers,
looking wise, if the notes are flat and hard—and every
now and then really false?

The violin begins. The singing begins.

Siv bends her head in shame.

But he *does* know mathematics.

The first lessons were spent on equations and square
roots, the following ones on conversions and logarithms.

Siv dresses up for her lessons. Her hair is brushed, she
dabs perfume behind her ears, and her blouse is pushed
tightly down into her skirt so that the little bit of woman's
body which she has acquired can be displayed most ad-
vantageously.

She sits bent over her father's desk. Svend is sitting on
the edge of the desk. They are alone in the room.

Siv turns, looks up at the young man who kindly, help-
fully and with endless patience repeats and corrects.

She looks at his powerful legs, at his thighs which seem
even stronger pressed against the edge of the desk.

They are really too large, she thinks. Men's thighs are
not supposed to be that large. But then what does she
know about such things? It is really a matter of taste.
They are not handsome when they are too thin, are they?

She wants to let her hand glide up his leg, right over
his knee, to bore her fingers into his practical knickers,
to shock him, tickle him, to drive her fingertips hard up-
wards, along the inside of his thighs, putting her nails
in—ah—h—h! He couldn't be pure mathematics right
down to his big toe, could he?

"Really, Siv, you don't seem to be listening."

"No!" she slowly admits.

"You look as if you're thinking of something completely different. Your thoughts are far away."

She raises her head, smiles and looks into his eyes. "No."

He looks at her, somewhat embarrassed. "Oh, yes, they
are. Pull yourself together now."

She groans, "I'm not going to be an accountant, you
know!"

"No."

"Nor am I going to be an engineer."

"No."

"I'll never have any use for all this. It's just a waste of time."

He shakes his head, patronizingly. "That's not the point. You've got to learn it so that you can pass your exams and get your diploma. You've got to go through with it; you might as well accept the fact."

She nods her head with feigned gentleness, turns again to her book and notepad. Mixed up with her own messy scratchings are fine, neat calculations—Svend's brave attempts to impress her with the "method" by which it is done.

She feels a sneaking madness in her body. It begins in her fingers, it tingles ceaselessly in them, it sucks at her stomach in impatience. She twists her legs together, feeling a familiar, tickling sensation low in her abdomen. She throws down her pencil and stretches her fingers.

Svend sits with a notepad about to write down a new problem.

She looks at him with wonder. The sun is shining outside. Last Sunday she found her first edelweiss in the wood. Everything smells of spring, growth, life.

She can feel the spring through the open window, hear it in the busy traffic, smell it, touch it, taste it.

And this young man just sits here preoccupied with a math problem? It is almost too incredible to be believed!

She stretches her arms over her head and lets one of her hands fall down on his thigh with a little hard smack.

He looks at her with surprise, blushes a little. "What's the matter?"

She repeats, somewhat irritated, "What's the matter? Well, I can't *stand* sitting here any longer. I've got to get out into the sunshine."

He shakes his head. "We have to finish your lesson first. And remember that I'm being paid to help you, so I have to try."

"We can tell Mother that I've got a headache, and then we can go for a walk."

She smiles persuasively, collecting all the beams at her command, sending them out through her eyes, mouth and the whole of her pliant face, offering her eagerness with laughing hands.

He is—in spite of everything—more than just mathematics. It is just that mathematics controls him, while the fireworks from an irrational young girl confuse and embarrass him.

He hops down from the desk, clears his throat a bit bashfully, occupies himself with straightening up the books. "Do what you like. You know it doesn't matter to me whether you pass your exam or not."

Siv jumps up from the desk and sits on the spot Svend has just vacated. It is still warm from his body. "Can't you come with me?"

"Of course I can."

She giggles: Yes, of course he can. All he has to do is put one foot in front of the other.

He looks up, embarrassed and annoyed. "What's the matter?"

"Nothing at all!" And she hops down from the desk. "Nothing—nothing—absolutely nothing at all!"

They go for a walk. Siv on her long, thin legs, and Svend with his student cap on his blonde hair and with a dawning infatuation in his eyes.

Svend's noble efforts are successful beyond all expectations. Siv gets her diploma and surprises both herself and her teacher by making a good grade in mathematics.

Summer and autumn have passed and winter has arrived. Siv is home all day helping her mother in the house while they think about what she is to do for a living.

Both her father and mother want to keep their child for a little while longer, and Siv has no idea what she would like to learn—perhaps nursing, but she is still too young for that.

Svend is often in Siv's home, where he has become an esteemed and honored guest. Her mother is especially fond of him. He plays the piano and sings about "Silver threads among the gold." He sings with a deep, soft trained voice, and her mother sits, touched, in a rocking chair looking up at his broad back.

Sometimes Siv is bored, answers irritably and tosses her feet impatiently or interrupts the singing with an uncalled-for remark.

Ino looks at her with surprise and reproach. Afterwards, she sometimes speaks to Siv alone, trying to capture her eyes. "Are you really aware of what a splendid young man Svend is, and that he is very fond of you? Sometimes you act so strangely when he's here that I can't understand what gets into you. Your father and I are so very fond of him, you know."

Her father and mother, of course! And God probably is, too—but what about Siv?

Well, she likes him, as far as that is concerned. He is a man. He is grown, wise and well-read. He is also rich and when he gets older, they will surely get engaged.

He sits on the bench in the kitchen with his legs crossed, smiling at Siv and her mother, and his teeth are large and shiny white.

Whenever he discovers that the water bucket is empty, he gets up and goes out to fill it, comes back in and sets it down on the white scoured bench without spilling a drop.

He walks over to her mother, putting a hand on her shoulder, while explaining to her about a dish which his own mother makes and which is particularly delicious.

He sits down again on the bench, blinking his big, heavy eyebrows a little, smiling warmly at Siv, setting his elbows on the table and bending his long fingers so that the knuckles crack.

There are so many things about him that Siv does not like. She is not quite sure precisely what they are and does everything she can to avoid finding out.

He follows all the rules. His shoes are always shined, almost varnished, but the heavy weave of his jacket material and pants keep him from looking like a snob.

And Siv senses that he is good, that he does not just wish to be, but that he *is* good. She tries to forget his awkward, unsure movements, the way he cracks his knuckles, the way he plays the violin for the congregation. And she looks into the kind, gray eyes which shine at her with cautious tenderness, with warmth and admiration.

Everyone longs for tenderness, true tenderness. Everyone needs it. One can manage to live without it, but everyone walks around with a yearning for tenderness shouting inside him.

And for someone like Siv, the need for tenderness is very great.

Yes, the lonelier you are inside, the more you yearn for human contact and understanding. You kick and fight your way through to another person's hands, to love, to a closeness which you are never able to find, especially if you are one of those persons who happen to be "different."

But Siv does not want to be "different." She harbors no wish for that. Svend is normal, boundlessly normal and good. She will try to come close to him, to merge herself with the reasonable and calm things of life. She will shake off all her strange dreams and desires which are of no use in the everyday world and which surely exist only in dreams.

She will try. God help her, how much she wants to— but *cannot*.

One evening she follows Svend to the garden gate. She stands holding onto the handlebars of his bicycle, looking up at him—questioningly.

She stands in a sleeveless knitted sweater, shivering a little from the cold, straightens up and relaxes her body. It is so nice every now and then to let the cold penetrate all your pores, so that your skin becomes cold and numb.

It is a dark evening, and Siv, too, is dark—and enticingly soft and young. Svend looks at her hand resting on his bicycle, sees the dark eyes shining hotly in the muted light— and he carefully puts his hand on hers.

Siv pulls her hand away and walks up to him, unbuttons his jacket, puts her arms around his body and snuggles up close to him.

He is a little at a loss, but enjoys it and puts his jacket around her.

She murmurs, "Mmmm!" She grinds herself in between his legs, hides her face in his neck and suddenly thinks it strange that he has never kissed her. So she looks up at him, all aglow and tempting—and continues to grind.

He grabs her around her waist and pushes her away, buttoning up his jacket. His face quivers with love and embarrassment. "There, you silly child, be a good girl."

She stands there shivering after her journey into the warm jacket. She feels somewhat betrayed and disappointed. But she is quite aware of the fact that she has done something wrong. Svend has behaved correctly, exactly as her father and mother expect him to behave.

Siv does not forget how she is to behave for the rest of the winter, at any rate not during the day or in the evening when Svend is visiting. She forgets, sometimes, at night, but only God sees that. Siv comforts herself with the thought that sometimes He might be too busy to pay any attention to her burning fantasies in the dark or the rocking motions she makes with her body until she experiences a mental rape which sucks her up into heaven and down to hell.

It could happen, every now and then, that God might be too busy.

CHAPTER SEVEN

And Siv becomes engaged.

The whole thing happens very quietly. She glides from the embrace of friendship into the embrace of an engagement without any uneasiness or big changes.

Svend buys her a wide engagement ring; Siv lets it glide on her finger, looking as if she is possessed by this serious symbol and feels adult and wise.

She has arrived unscathed and happy after her trip around dangerous reefs. Her father and mother nod affectionately to them. The congregation nods affectionately to them. Two young people, following the same path, the path to heaven, the Savior's path. And they look so nice together, Svend—tall, strong, blonde, and Siv—tiny, dark and delicate.

Of course, they are very young, especially Siv, who is only sixteen years old. Svend, on the other hand, is twenty-two. But it will work out all right. They are in love with each other and have the same God. By now Svend has kissed her. He kisses her gently, with closed lips. They take walks together, go to prayer meeting together and look into the same hymnal.

Siv wants to be a nurse. Svend is studying to be a doctor. A delightful couple! They talk together about their future. They want to help each other, complement each other. Perhaps it is God's will that they might travel someday as missionaries, teaching the heathen about God. They will help them, cure and nurse them.

Svend looks at Siv with enchantment. No one can look so warmly at her as Svend does. Behind his thick eye-glasses, his soft, gray eyes are dark with warmth. His glance envelops her tiny, pretty body, and in a rush of infatuated confusion, he sees her as God's marvelous gift: a truly beautiful, little woman, whom other men desire, but who, just the same, is to be *his* and only his. He has found both a pious woman and an enticing, erotic woman. Yes, imagine, he has actually found her. These two things are united in Siv's being.

One day he will be given authority over this girl whom other men observe so admiringly. All the other men will have to forget their desires, resign, retreat, because she is a Christian, his Siv, and his alone.

Svend is happy, very happy. Every time he meets Siv he has some small gift for her, rational, useful things, nothing too expensive, no, such things would not suit them.

They decide what pattern of silverware they are going to set their table with some day, and Svend saves his pocket money and buys sometimes one, at other times three spoons or forks. He also buys small lamps, tablecloths, an electric mixer, a sewing table and an embroidery frame.

His father is wealthy, but is a rational man, who gives Svend little pocket money. His son is to learn to know the value of money.

And Svend agrees with his father. Svend's relationship to his parents is reasonable, calm and open. The ideal family relationship, the sort one reads about. Siv is enchanted by all of this, conquered.

No one—no one—will ever find out what she is really like inside. She will have to live up to all of this. She should be grateful for everything. She will have a safe and calm life. Her father and mother have decided on it, and so have Svend's father and mother—and so has Svend.

Of course, she will. That is what everybody is trying to achieve, isn't it? As a rule, then, she is quiet and thoughtful: So this is to be her life?

But it happens that, when she walks through the streets together with Svend, she encounters other eyes. It happens that, when she stands in the bath in the evening, stroking the washcloth over her body, she enjoys it and thinks: "This body is promised to Svend alone. Will he be able to value it?"

What pride! She winces a bit, but the thoughts continue. "How delightful I am! Heavens! How delightful I am!"

She stands up on her toes, then climbs on the bathroom stool so that she can also see her legs in the mirror. She strokes herself across her stomach, plays a bit with her black tuft of hair, stretches and turns: All of them should see her now, all of them who only guess when they see her on the street. Is all this really to be Svend's?

If she now—without anyone's finding it out, without anything's happening—if she could show this to another man, an experienced man, to hear his judgment?

She hops quickly down from the stool, dries herself, fastens her bra about her breasts after a final look. She sighs and is a little ashamed: Why does she wish—that *others* could see her?

But she does wish it. She has wished it with a hidden, painful yearning throughout all the years of her youth. She wants to be seen by men. She wants others to observe her, evaluate her, others to desire her. She longs for all this with a burning need, while she takes walks with Svend like an honorable, faithful and engaged virgin.

She looks at absolutely every man they pass. She captures every glance, sucking into herself all of their admiration. And if a man walks past her unmoved, she feels herself to be betrayed and lonely. She looks at their shoulders, their hands and hips, their gait, the expression of their eyes and the cast of their mouths. She watches to see whether they turn to look back at her. She looks honorably at the ground, trying to hide her smile of triumph. But there is something behind her closed lips which ripples the trembling corners of her mouth and gives her face a look of sensual knowledge.

Svend becomes erotic when walking with her. One could hardly expect anything else. Her thoughts and wishes capture him.

After all, he is going to be a doctor, learn anatomy, conditions, learn *everything*—in theory.

He begins to talk about this theory. Siv understands him with a hidden evil.

He talks about everything: stimulation, copulation and orgasm. The man's duty to understand the woman, her desires and sensations, about where the various nerve centers are located, about perversions and variations.

He looks so wise as he talks. As he walks, he looks modestly and contentedly at the ground, squeezes her hand —is very professional.

Siv's heart, mind, and senses leap with unrest and impatience. Everyone else discovers all of these things, Svend—everyone else. They discover all of this even though they are not studying to become doctors, don't they?

But Svend does not dare, will not, has no right to. He talks—and talks. Every now and then he looks at Siv, shyly from the side.

She is waiting!

He is the man. He is the one who will have to do something, isn't he?

But Svend only takes her hand, squeezes it, talks about their home, their children. And blood streams from Siv's throat, down through her breasts, into her abdomen and legs so that she feels herself made impotent from longing and confusion: so long, much too long, to have to wait. Two, three, four years—perhaps still more?

She does not know any theory about nerves. She just has them in her body. She listens to him seriously and with curiosity, questioning him every now and then, glancing into his face, sits down on a bench and lets her dress glide up above her knees, puts her hand between her legs while grabbing Svend's thigh with her other hand. She looks nervously at him, bites through his shirt, kisses him on his neck. "What about the animals, Svend? They can't read."

He embraces her and kisses her. A kiss? There is also something about that in those books he has read.

He carefully opens his mouth, tries to stick his tongue into Siv's mouth. She quickly pulls back: it is so nasty, because there is something wrong somewhere, something completely wrong. What is there so wrong with his just now *trying* to do it right?

And so it goes, day in and day out, for weeks, months, years.

Something is wrong—with what?

Siv finally thinks she knows what is the matter: There is something wrong with her. There always has been, so there is nothing to be done about it. She will have to hide it, just as she has always done.

There is always something inside a person which must be kept hidden from others, isn't there? Yes, she is almost sure of it, and this comforts her.

CHAPTER EIGHT

The war is still going on out in the world as well as in Denmark.

Svend takes part in the war—verbally.

When he visits Siv he tries to pick up the broadcasts from the English radio, curses the German interference which prevents him from hearing clearly, makes comments, slaps his thighs, becomes excited and annoyed.

He is tall and strong, filling the entire room with his healthy, sports-trained body, striding back and forth across the the carpet, running his fingers through his closely cut, curly hair which always looks so neat. His skin is pink and white like a young girl's, his lips are red, large and plump, in front of his shiny white teeth. He does not smoke; he does not drink. My God! How healthy he is. Is there anything the matter with him? No, there can't be.

He has been a Boy Scout. He began as a Cub Scout when he was little and ended up as a troop leader. He speaks with a big, warm smile about "my boys!" There is no flag so beautiful as the Danish flag, no land so good and orderly as Denmark. There is no father so witty as his and no mother so good and sacrificing.

And in the whole history of the world, there has never been such an evil and bestial race as the Germans.

Everything the English say is the pure, absolute truth, everything the Germans say is lies and propaganda.

On such evenings Siv thinks that he is stupid, very stupid. It is obvious that you can find scoundrels and liars everywhere. They can be found in England as well as in Germany. Siv thinks that the best thing you can do is to base your total picture on a sum gathered from both sides, subtracting a half from what each says, mix that which remains and find the common denominator.

It is just a question of mathematics, isn't it?

She sits mocking Svend in her heart, keeping quiet most of the time, but mocking him with an anger which has no reasonable cause whatsoever. For *if* he really hated, she could respect him. Love and hate, genuine and total, Siv understands such things. But Svend is angry only because that is how all good Danes are supposed to feel—for the time being. He yells without doing anything, like everyone else. He sits rejoicing and hopping up and down when German towns are destroyed and is idiotically furious when it happens to be London's turn.

But in all the nations at war—in Germany and England, America, Russia, Japan—completely innocent people are being killed every day, just because idiots like Svend are— so patriotic! That is how it looks to Siv. That is her feminine, nonprofessional view of war and politics, and the result is that she can no longer keep quiet.

She becomes a shocking political commentator in the yellow house.

Her father does not take part in the discussions; he just smiles patronizingly. Her mother looks as if she does not understand. And Svend rages.

He gets angry with Siv, the girl he loves and admires with a melting tenderness.

More soldiers come to town. Svend tells how they stuff themselves at the bakery with cakes filled with cream: "The way they come up here and eat up our food! You should have seen how disgusting it was to see them standing there stuffing themselves."

Siv then asks him with a thin, kind voice, "Svend, do you want me to go down to the bakery to buy you some cakes filled with cream?"

He answers, without thinking, "No, thank you. I don't like that kind of cake."

"But, Svend, if you don't like cakes filled with cream, what difference does it make if the Germans eat them?"

"Oh, Siv, you don't understand anything! They're using us as a pantry."

"Maybe, Svend. But we're not starving. We get enough to eat, don't we?"

"Yes!" says Svend. His face is red, and he tightens his

mouth, looking terrible, because of the unusual bags in the corners of his mouth which make him look as if he always has a piece of candy in each side of his mouth.

And Siv says with a deep, amused voice, "It's a well-stocked pantry!"

Her father laughs, and her mother says nervously, "There, there!"

And Svend walks angrily back and forth across the floor, with a red face and violent steps.

Siv cannot refrain from continuing, "We Danes were too fat anyway."

Svend turns to her, asking indignantly, "Do you find all these ration stamps so funny?"

"No, but all the other countries have them—and not as many as we have, by a long shot." She begins to be angry. "Oh, all these complaints about things that don't matter!"

Svend says without motivation, "The Norwegians are starving!"

"Yes," answers Siv, "the Norwegians are starving, and they are also mad at the Germans, because they fought, and you have to be mad to fight. But the Danes didn't fight. They gave up in advance because they were afraid of getting a beating. They've no reason to feel sorry for themselves."

She gets support from her father, who nods his head. Svend looks from one to the other, becomes unsure of himself, which only makes him angrier.

"You sound like a bunch of Nazis!"

Her father laughs quietly. Siv smiles maliciously and Svend wraps his scarf about his throat and leaves.

But he comes back the following day, pulls Siv close to him and says, blushing and with emotion, "I've thought over what happened yesterday, and I think you're right." This is even worse. She twists herself out of his arms, nods forgiveness, and hastily thinks of other things.

But a few days later things go wrong again.

An air-raid signal is blown while they are drinking their evening coffee. The yellow house has its own air-raid shelter in the cellar.

When they arrive at the cellar door, they find three German woman telegraphists standing there. They are unable to get back to their camp in time and ask if they may be allowed to go into the cellar. One cannot say no.

Her father shows them to a bench.

Svend walks up and down the room. He will not look at anyone, neither the German girls nor the Esruth family.

Siv enjoys herself. This is just what he needs.

One of the ladies sits uneasily and finally gets up and walks over to Ino, saying something to her. Her mother looks confusedly at her. She does not understand German. She looks nervously at Svend, but he *won't* understand German.

It dawns on Siv that the woman wants to go to the toilet. She nods and shows her the way out to the yard. She returns to the cellar, looking with pleasure at Svend's ridiculous, angry face: Does he really hate them? Has she misjudged him?

The woman returns. A quarter of an hour passes before the all-clear is sounded.

The German women nod a polite farewell, the others walk into the house. Svend rushes into the kitchen, grabs one of her mother's kettles which is always boiling on the stove and runs out into the yard with it.

Siv follows him with curiosity: What is he going to do?

She walks over to the well-kept outhouse—Svend is standing there about to throw the boiling water on the toilet seat.

Siv asks sharply, "What are you thinking of doing?"

He blushes deeply, straightens up and looks at her. "There can be all sorts of things wrong with these German WAC's. I don't want you to come here afterwards and catch anything."

"You don't, do you?" Siv explodes. She flies at Svend, tears the kettle out of his hand, throws it out into the yard, and while he stands there frozen with astonishment, pulls up her dress and pulls down her pants. She sits down on the toilet seat and hisses, "Get out. I prefer being alone, if you don't mind. What an idiot you are!"

Svend flees and laughter bubbles up in Siv. That showed him—showed him who was the stronger! But how ridiculous the whole thing is!

How can she stay engaged to such a super idiot who believes that all Germans are devils with terrible diseases and all Englishmen are angels.

But she continues to be engaged to Svend. They do not always talk about war, and every time they have a violent argument, Svend always comes the next day, kisses her and makes up.

CHAPTER NINE

Siv and Svend are alone one evening in the yellow house. Her father and mother are out visiting a family also in the congregation.

They sit in the room Siv calls "the cozy room," the room where her father's violin hangs on the wall and where his desk is. This is the room they go to after they have eaten supper in the kitchen, the room with deep, worn easy chairs and a wide sofa and two windows which face the street and the sea. It is a room where you do not have to be proper, just comfortable.

There is also the dining room, and the best parlor, which is heated up only when guests are expected. Siv cannot stand that room, and it seems as if nobody else can, either. But it *has* to be there, without a speck of dust, without worn chairs and the smell of people.

But Siv and Svend are sitting in the most comfortable room. Svend has brought his books over, but it does not look as if he will get any reading done.

They have been discussing their future, what they will do when they get their own home. Enchanted by the thought, Svend looks at Siv with a warm, protective glance in his eyes.

He will never be able to be strict with her. Her wishes are his law. He will make every effort to give her a good home, a comfortable home, the bathroom with black tiles that she wants.

And he will come home every Saturday with flowers, and they will spend their Sundays in perfect bliss.

They will go visiting their parents, perhaps, some time in the future, with a child in their arms, a little child that says "Daddy" and "Mommy"—and everything will be just perfect!

Siv remembers her earlier childhood. It was warm and

safe. She remembers the closeness and the companionship. Yes, that is just the way she wants her child to experience it. Because the most important thing in life is to love your fellowman and enrich one another's lives.

Svend is lying on the sofa with his hands behind his neck. He sends a broad and blissful smile to Siv. They have talked about so many good things, and there is a closeness, a contact between them.

Siv sits on the edge of the sofa, her hand gliding up over his sweater. She embraces him around his neck. She sighs, stretches herself out, and lies next to him, swinging her legs up, pressing closely against him. She buries her face in his neck, sniffing the warmth and smell of his body.

Now she lies flat on top of him with her abdomen on his, against the hard, buttoned-up fly of his trousers, her legs locked in his.

Siv begins to move her body, very gently at first, but later with more and more violence. She raises her chest and pushes her belly hard and tightly against him. She rocks, swings, clucks and laughs: Svend suddenly has such a funny expression on his face.

He grabs her and carefully pushes her away. "Don't do that!" But there is no strength in his hands, no noticeable will.

And so Siv continues. She looks at Svend, her fiancé, the handsome young man who has never admitted that he, too, has sensation, and, driven by feelings which are part bliss, part revenge, she moves her body in increasingly passionate circles, crushes, screws, kisses him on his neck, bites.

Svend says once again, "Don't!" But his face is red and ecstatic and he does not push her away.

She continues with her close, fully dressed embrace, sees Svend's face fill with shame, feels something warm and wet on her belly, moves over and sees a wet stain on his trousers.

She jumps up, looking at him with triumph. She does not say a word, but thinks to herself: "I showed him. In spite of everything, he's just a man, even though he won't admit it."

Svend gets up, blushing, walks quickly past her, out of the room and into the bathroom.

Siv sits down in a chair still tingling with desire: So, you've come, haven't you? Oh, yes, it's all over for you!

But what about me? It's not over for me—you're supposed to make me come, too!

She sits, feeling pains in her stomach, jabbing pains which kill all feelings of desire: Why can't—I—also experience that which is completely wonderful? Why don't you help me, since you love me and we are going to get married?

Svend comes in again, sits down, embarrassed, and looks at her.

Siv bows her head, hiding her talkative eyes, because she feels a hate so strong and incomprehensible at this moment that she does not believe that she will be able to control herself. Her body and soul are on fire and her thoughts are not clear: I could pick up something in my hand and smash him. Then I'd be free. Then I'd be a criminal, but I'd surely be able to find a man before the police captured me.

But she looks at his unhappy, shy, masculine head and becomes her normal self once more: It is terrible what she can think and feel, isn't it? Svend cannot help it if she goes crazy every now and then. He is innocent, he is good.

She stands up and sighs, runs her fingers through his hair and walks out of the room to stir up the fire and put the coffee on.

Her father and mother will probably be home soon.

CHAPTER TEN

Siv has lived at home with her father and mother for nineteen years. She has helped her mother in the house, she has been fed, clothed and corrected. She has been labeled a good young girl.

She has become a member of the choir. She plays a lute and sings the Holy One's songs. But she also plays amusing things on her lute, letting her fingers glide up and down at an insane tempo, making trembling rhythms between the beats.

She lifts her chin and sings with her husky, dark voice, sings out her longing for life in words about God and the Holy Ghost.

Mr. Rasmussen, the director of the choir, is very interested in Siv. He is interested in her musical talent and her dark voice.

She attends the prayer meetings, is on her knees for several hours praying to God. She speaks to Him, wildly and imploringly. She begs that He satisfy her, fill her with strength and the Holy Ghost.

She shifts uncomfortably on her knees, looking at the long row of kneeling people, most of whom are women.

The director of the choir is also the leader for the prayer meetings. He is a handsome man. He is dark with soft, brown eyes, a sharp, straight nose and a small, sensitive mouth.

Siv looks at the row of humble women with their broad behinds. She watches as the leader walks around laying his hand on their necks, praying together with them so that they get a "shock." They move their broad behinds, shake their shoulders, shout out "in tongues" all their enthusiasm for God and His glory.

Watching this, Siv completely loses the holy excitement which she felt earlier. Her soul is nauseous. She gets strange, sensual thoughts. If only these women had small, nice behinds! But they are so ugly!

She hides her face in her hands, prays to God to free her from sinful thoughts. She screams and calls on God as though calling after a faithless lover.

Some evenings there is "free testimony." Now and then Siv stands up on these evenings. She walks up to the wide platform in order to proclaim her faith before all men.

She enjoys looking into all these upturned, expectant faces.

She stands by the rostrum, slender and dark, with fanatic, agonized eyes. She speaks without a text—but she speaks well!

She knows it, too!

"It is written in the Bible that it is easier for a camel to pass through the eye of a needle than it is for a rich man to enter the kingdom of Heaven!

"That is the way it is if you are too wise. If you insist on being too wise. You are to restrain your thoughts, have a childish and naïve faith. There is so much talk today about how you ought to widen your horizon. You are supposed to read, learn, become wise and know all things.

"It sounds enticing, but *if you want to be a Christian,* it is a grave danger. Because then you start trying to figure out God's ways, and no one can understand God. We can only feel him!

"So, if you want to get into heaven, if you want to come safely into port, avoiding all tempting thoughts and theories—then you have to believe in God, unconditionally, childishly and naïvely."

Siv's cheeks burn, and she sings out her convulsive faith.

And she is wonderful standing there defending her belief.

The older speakers nod to each other with approval: Here is faith and passion. The leader bows his head and says amen.

Siv sees it out of the corners of her eyes, with eyes that have always rolled as though on double ballbearings. She sees it and feels secure within her soul. She is pious, she is spiritual. Sacho's God has not forsaken her. She is filled to the brim with spiritual wisdom.

And she goes home after the meeting, subduing the screaming "no" in her soul with the joy and tenderness she gets from her father and mother, with the pride and love she gets from Svend.

Things are really beginning to work out as they should for her.

But Siv has to leave home. She has to go away and learn something. Her father has decided that this is the best, and she agrees. She wants to go away, to see new things.

She wants to become a nurse. It has now been decided; that is what she will do.

There are still a few years to go before Svend will be through with his education, before they can get married.

Her father pushes Siv down into a chair, looks seriously at her. "Siv, you've got to learn something, so that you'll be able to manage whatever might happen."

Siv nods and smiles as a warm, silent current of under-standing flows from father to daughter. Siv believes that she can hear what he is thinking:

"Well, we won't talk any more about it, but we're both sinners. Perhaps you're not as strong as I am. You're a woman, and women haven't been given such strong wills as men.

"Who knows how things will work out? Will Svend be your life insurance? It's best that you insure your own life."

Ino enters the room. She walks over to Siv. "Have you two decided whether you are to leave home?"

"Yes!" Siv turns away from her mother's arms. She looks at her father.

He observes them both with a friendly and loving look.

Father and mother and daughter.

And that is the way things should be, Siv. This is what makes life pleasant. It is only that your feelings are too strong and therefore wrong.

You are the child of *both*, not just Sacho's darling!

You, Siv, who cannot look at a man, not even your own father, without being painfully aware of the fact—that he is a man!

CHAPTER ELEVEN

You are familiar with the hospital.

You know that it is the red building in the center of town. Between three and four o'clock a thick stream of people floods through the gates to visit sick friends.

You know the smell in the white corridors which you have seen when you yourself were paying a visit.

You have seen the white-clad nurses walking down the hall with an unapproachable stiffness in their faces and aprons.

Perhaps you have also been a patient and have experienced the rules and regulations, the friendliness and good care.

And yet you don't know the hospital.

A hospital is a world which embraces all of humanity: happy tears when a child is born, crushing sorrow at death, quiet resignation, burning hope, greatness and pitiable weakness.

A hospital is all this—and much, much more.

It is also laughter, rejoicing young laughter.

The hospital is full of young girls. They come from all classes of society, but they all have to do the same work: look after the sick, stand erect like soldiers before the head nurse, listen to complaints, confidential whispers, and do the most nonesthetic work which is reserved especially for the young newcomers.

The result is a solidarity, a marvelous comradeship.

The girls stand together, with all their frivolous curiosity and ignorance, their youth and bubbling laughter.

A gossiping, twittering army against illness and a patient's gloomy thoughts.

It is a good thing that this is the way it is, both for the sick and for the girls as well. Some day they will have heard too many screams, seen too much which could have been done differently, understood too much.

But not yet!

Siv is shown to her room in the nurse's dormitory, a long three-storied building. The rooms line long halls, side by side, with a few yards' distance between each door. They are all the same: small and narrow and furnished with a bed covered with a green blanket, green curtains, a table of light oak with a matching chair, an armchair, a little night table and a bookshelf.

Siv is given a room on the second floor, number two hundred and six.

And she is happy! It does not matter that her room is little, that it is just like all the other rooms on the hall, that the walls are so thin that she can hear most of the sounds from the adjoining rooms, that there is a common toilet and common kitchenette. It does not matter at all, it is just delightful. Because otehr young girls live in the other rooms, they meet in the hallways, in the kitchen or stand in line outside the bath waiting their turn. There is laughter and comradeship, blazing dressing gowns and buttoned-up uniforms. There is whispering and giggling, noisy record players and the tripping sounds of high-heeled shoes.

In the evenings they meet in their rooms, squeezing together in the nut-sized, cosy rooms, solving all the problems of the world, talking disrespectfully about the strict head nurses. They listen to one another's problems, give good advice, tell about their sweethearts, about kisses and embraces, dances and new dresses.

There are definite rules for the nurse's dormitory: you have to be in before twelve o'clock at night, and if you have guests, they have to be out before twelve.

The house mother must be a little stupid if she believes that these regulations are able to protect their holy virtue. Some are engaged, like Siv, and wear shiny rings; others are "in the market." They are the most interesting. They always have so much to tell. They know the bars and restaurants, know men and their silly desires, know life!

At least Siv thinks so, and she listens with interest and a secret envy. She does not tell her colleagues that she is still a virgin, a girl who has been engaged since she was fifteen years old. That would have embarrassed her. She takes in all the conversations and her inspired imagination helps her. The result is that her colleagues believe that she is the worst of them all.

What fun it all is, and she almost experiences what she tells as she tells it.

They are good comrades. Siv has never experienced such comradeship.

The girls who live on the first floor help the others out by leaving their windows open if they come home too late. Ecstatic and filled with the night's adventures, the girls climb over the rose bushes, which tear their stockings to pieces. They find their friend's room, climb in and take off their clothes so that they look as if they have just been to the toilet. Perhaps they also borrow a nightgown which has been laid out for this purpose. They wrap a towel over their party dress and high-heeled shoes, sneak out of the door, past the wide-awake guards, and up to their rooms, proud of this successful criminal expedition.

It is a happy world Siv has entered.

And her ward? Yes, of course, it can be a little difficult.

When you are new, you make many mistakes. But you have no responsibility, you do not have to be able to do anything. If you are bawled out, you just have to go to the washroom and pour out the injustice to a compassionate colleague. The devil take those old hags! They have no idea what it means to be alive, as old and ugly as they are. They have no part at all in the happy world where young girls laugh.

They must have been young, too, once upon a time. Every now and then Siv thinks about this. Yes, they must have been young once, but that was a long, long time ago.

Siv has not been on the ward for more than two days when a death occurs.

She looks at the eyes of those concerned, which are red from tears, and rushes away.

So it can be a serious thing to be a nurse.

After the family has gone, the body must be prepared.

An older nurse, Miss Svendsen, comes into the kitchen where Siv and her sister nurses are fixing their evening snack.

She stands there a while looking at them, then she nods to Siv:

"Come with me to room nine."

Siv follows calmly.

They walk into the room, put on white coats and stand one on each side of the bed.

The cold, dead eyes look right at Siv. She shivers.

Miss Svendsen hastily closes them, looking curiously at Siv. Siv's eyes meet hers, and she sees that they are warm and concerned. They ask if this is too much for her. They know that Siv is very young, just over nineteen years old. These eyes, with their thick, heavy bags hanging over her cheeks, have seen a good deal.

Siv smiles carefully and reassuringly to her, and she regrets everything she has ever said about old nurses.

Miss Svendsen bends over the bed, showing Siv what is to be done, her voice is calm and ordinary:

"Next, we have to do this, Miss Esruth. The clothing must be removed—yes, and afterwards the body is to be washed."

Most of the time Siv just stands there watching and is not of much use, but she understands now that that is not why she is there. Miss Svendsen took her in with her because she is the youngest, because she wants to help this young girl over her first experience with death.

The room is quiet. No complaints. No heavy, painful breathing, as there had been when Siv had been in this room before. There is no crying family, no lamentations, just a white, quiet body, a face which looks peaceful and relaxed, almost beautiful now that the eyes have been closed.

It cannot be so hard to die then?

Miss Svendsen places wet wads of cotton over the eyelids so that they will remain closed. She ties a towel tightly under the chin so that the jaw will not fall open.

Siv looks at Miss Svendsen—and likes her.

She has done this many times before, yet there is respect and reverence in her careful movements, a warmth in her tired face. Every now and then she glances kindly at Siv, and Siv returns her glance with open, shiny eyes and remains very calm.

Siv understands her, understands that she, too, will learn to handle a dead body with care, because this body has lived and has been loved.

Miss Svendsen hastily runs her fingers through the dead,

clammy hair, places a sheet over the body, walks over to
the window and opens it, takes Siv by the arm and shoves
her before her out of the door:

"Thanks for helping me."

It rushes through Siv: Thanks for helping? It is she who
should say thanks. She does not look at Miss Svendsen;
she walks in the opposite direction down the corridor. But
she places Miss Svendsen solidly and deeply in her uneasy
heart.

In the years that come, Siv discovers that there are many
ways in which to prepare the dead.

CHAPTER TWELVE

Siv has begun in a male ward.

It is not a good thing.

They speak of nurses as the third sex, or neuter in gender.

Of course, you are allowed to be a woman in private, but once you put on your white uniform, the tight-fitting apron and the starched cap—well, you are a nurse!

A man does not have to be ashamed of his nakedness, because a nurse is to have calm, professional eyes which see only the patient, not the man.

That is the way things are, and that is the way they should be! Siv, however, is not able to remove her sex when she removes her street clothes.

She has become quite good at the manual work, because she has practical, strong hands, but she spreads uneasiness, brings confusion into the hospital, which is otherwise so strict and well-organized.

With great difficulty she has managed to gather her long, dark hair up on her head. It sits up there, a loose, luxuriant crown into which her cap disappears. She looks like a prancing circus pony when she comes dancing across the corridor with her narrow face beneath the towering mass of hair, with her nervous, smiling, uneasy eyes and an apron which almost goes twice around her narrow waist.

She seals her large, soft mouth over her youth and tingling curiosity, holds her neck high and tries to look noble.

Her most difficult problem is her eyes! The only way she can control them is not to look at anyone too long. She lets them roam from the one to the other, dashes out of the door while looking at the wall or the washbasin. But she thinks that all the men in their beds, young and old, watch her, that they know things which no one must know, that they do not think of her as a nurse.

It often happens that she forgets herself, completely forgets that a nurse is to be respectable and reserved.

A young patient asks her to shake his pillow and turn the cool side up.

She willingly says yes, stands there thoughtfully, shaking, beating, glancing at the pillow, turning it: Which side was the cool side, I wonder?

She smiles at the man, puts her cheek to the pillow to feel which side is the coolest.

It is only afterwards, when she notices the blush on the man's face and hears the grunts of laughter from the other beds, that she wakes up and knows that you are not to do things like this! Her cheeks are not supposed to be warm and excited. She must not be coquettish.

The patient follows her with his warm eyes. She is afraid that they talk about her in the dayroom, that they amuse themselves at her expense—but that they are also fond of her. Haven't they a right to be fond of her?

Yes, but not in *that* way!

And yet! And yet she thinks it is very nice that they look at her differently from the way they look at the other nurse on the ward, Miss Knudsen. The way they groan and sigh, stretch out and grab her hands, holding them tightly with a shameless expression on their faces. Yes, it is just dreadful! But she takes it as a compliment!

And what about those solidly built, strong, healthy men who drive the ambulances—one of them, for example, who drinks beer in the kitchen and flirts with all of them. What if one of these men enters the washroom, the linen closet, or the kitchen when she is there? What if he grabs her hips from behind and pulls her to him so that she can feel him?

Well? However impudent one of them can be, she takes it as a compliment! She pretends to be annoyed, tears herself away and says, "Stop it!" But her mouth trembles into a smile and her eyes glisten with joy. The man laughs, sighs, shakes his head and tells her that she is damn sweet.

Smiling, Siv nods and disappears, but cannot manage to feel anything other than pride!

But she does not tell anybody else about these happenings, not even her sister nurses. They would surely find the whole thing too vulgar.

For she is engaged, and she walks around with her ring hanging on a string around her neck because they are not allowed to have such things on when on duty. When she is off-duty she can put it on so that everyone can see that she is engaged. They have also seen her sweetheart, and they think that he is handsome and looks very wise.

If they come into her room when Svend is there, they say hello and hurry out again.

Siv has given them the impression that she and Svend have tried *everything!* That Svend is very demanding in that area, and that every now and then she is completely exhausted and worn out by all of his demands.

Yes, her sister nurses understand this very well. They look at her with respect and admiration, and the girls who do not have boy friends look at her with envy.

But could Siv tell them how she enjoys all those other hands, how she soaks in all their glances and all their words, about how lovely she is? No, they would never be able to understand that. "But, Siv, you've got a boy friend, haven't you? The others are just trash, only fit for sluts!"

And what if they found out that she is a virgin, that she does not know anything more about love than what she has read and heard about? Then they would, and rightfully so, shrug their shoulders in contempt.

No, you don't tell everything, even to your best friends! She wears lipstick while on the ward, but if Svend comes to visit her in the evening, she rubs it off, and if she is to visit her father and mother, she brushes her hair smoothly away from her face and becomes an honorable, pious girl.

She still sings in the choir when she goes with her father and mother to meeting, but she no longer stands up and speaks when there is free testimony.

It also happens that she even forgets to say her evening prayers after she has lain down to go to sleep. There are so many other things to think about.

And her fear of God, Sacho's God?

Siv is no longer afraid. The first time you hear about something frightful, your soul turns cold with fear. But if you hear about the same thing time and time again, and if it begins to sound like some sort of threatening echo in your mind after so many years, then you learn to live with your fear. It becomes an old, familiar refrain. You put it away in a corner of your mind like a piece of trivial information. You accept it, but you cease being afraid of it, especially if you are, like Siv, walking around with the feeling that you can upset the whole world—just because you are young.

CHAPTER THIRTEEN

Peace returns to Denmark.

The Germans capitulate, everyone rejoices.

Siv is downtown the evening peace is declared. Bonfires are built in all the open places, people throw their blackout shades out of their windows. You can see flags and candles everywhere.

She watches two Danes trying to explain to a couple of German soldiers that it has been announced over the radio that Germany has surrendered, and that they can go home. They are at peace.

The Germans seem doubtful. Then they are shown a handbill which is translated into German for them. At least they dare believe the truth.

And then something happens which imprints itself deep in Siv's mind:

They throw their rifles down on the sidewalk, pull their steel helmets off of their furrowed faces and embrace the Danish men who told them the news. Now they can go home, back home, to see whether their families are still alive and whether their homes are still standing or have been destroyed by bombs.

They are going home, home, home, back home!

And they forget that Danes ought to hate them, and they embrace them. —

And blessed be these Danish men!

They do not gloat over the change. They are carried away by the warm communion which always ought to be felt between people. They ask each other about their families, and they all have a good time together.

During the days that follow, the hospital is a scene of spectacle and unrest.

The ambulances scream in carrying the men who do not dare face peace.

They have gassed themselves, taken poison or tried to hang themselves. Police stand beside their beds, and their doors are locked.

And down in the cellar the stretcher-bearers chase the washerwomen who have been German whores, "camp-beds."

"Siv, Siv, do you hear all the noise down in the cellar? Don't you want to go down and watch?"

She shakes her head and presses her lips together. "No!"

Poor girls. Most of them are ugly and stupid. They do not have many opportunities. But there were soldiers in town and these girls had their life's great adventure.

She does not want to watch their punishment. She would probably have attacked their executioners. And what would she be able to do? One girl against all those stretcher-bearers.

She gets reports from her colleagues. Twenty men are standing around a poor trembling girl waiting to shave her head! Yes, she thinks, she can see them in front of her: lots of patriotism in their mouths and lots of sadism in their trousers.

No, she is not going down into the cellar!

But the hair grows back on the heads of the girls who have been shaved. They give their short locks a permanent and dance gaily out to meet the English troops which have just arrived.

Nobody says anything about *that*.

But one day a girl is brought into the emergency room. She is dying, is operated on, but cannot be saved.

The patriots have turned her upside down and poured hydrochloric acid up her vagina. She had been a German whore.

Siv goes up to her room. She has a mascot, a fine Chinese doll. It sits on her divan in its colorful kimono, looking as if it knew everything. She picks it up and crushes it between her fingers so that the pieces of glass make deep wounds. Then she opens her window and throws it down into the rose bushes.

When Svend visits her that evening, she tells him what she has seen.

She stares stiffly at him: if he shows the slightest suggestion of approval of this thing which has happened, if he shrugs his shoulders and says that she got what she deserved—if he does this, then she will have nothing more to do with him.

"But, Svend, they're nothing but a bunch of pigs to do a thing like that, *pigs, pigs!* She was only sixteen years old —and beautiful."

Siv starts crying and the hard knot inside her brain begins to loosen. She looks imploringly up at Svend. "Don't you think that the whole thing is disgusting?"

She stretches her arms out toward him, is completely lost in her sorrow.

He takes two rapid steps over to her and crushes her against him, and says the redeeming words, "Yes, *that* was disgusting."

She can still continue to be engaged to him.

But whenever you find young people, you also find lively, bubbling laughter. This is the force that prevents their souls from rotting away in illness and misery. It rushes through everything. It flashes into the hospital and sits in a man's eye, in a girl's throat.

One night Siv hears uneasy and sneaky steps in the corridor.

She looks out. It is two interns. It is three in the morning, and they have been to a party and are now sneaking around the hall like two silly schoolboys up to no good.

What are they doing, I wonder?

She is on night duty, has been sitting enjoying herself with a book. She walks out to them. "Well, what in the world are you two doing?"

They look sternly at her. "Go back to your room. We'll come in minute or two."

One of them bends down, plucks a little blossom from a splendid basket of flowers which has been placed outside one of the doors, along with numerous other baskets of flowers.

"You've got to stop this. That's awful! Stealing the patients' flowers!"

She is deeply annoyed.

They look sadly at her, shake their heads in amazement. "We didn't think *you* were like that. We've only taken a little flower from each basket, and it doesn't even show."

"Well, what are you going to do with them?"

"They are for *you*, don't you understand? And you stand there giving us a hard time."

They look very injured. Siv manages to get them into the duty room.

"There you are!" The flowers shower over Siv's angry head.

They look at her expectantly. "Well, are you still mad at us?"

She cannot help laughing. She is not made to be strict, serious and to inspire respect.

"You are drunk, stinking drunk."

They deny this accusation heatedly.

"Why don't you two be nice boys and go home to bed?"

"Never."

Siv says maliciously, "Well, then, why don't you go down and visit 'Auntie.' "

"Auntie" is an older nurse who is on duty on the floor under them. There is an open pipe in the floor which runs down into the duty room below because the plumbers are in the process of rearranging the plumbing system.

"Oh, dear, old Auntie. Is she down there?"

The interns lie down on the floor and peer through the pipe. They look up at Siv with beams of joy. "She's sitting right under the pipe!"

And in spite of her wild protests, they begin to drop flowers through the pipe. She pulls and tugs at them. "You've got to stop that, you idiots. We'll get into trouble!"

But they are completely absorbed in their work. "You scored, did you see it?" They laugh, lying there, as big as they are, shoving the flowers down, peeking and shaking with laughter.

She cannot maintain her strict and serious attitude. The whole situation is so idiotic and ridiculous.

Here are two interns, usually so dignified, the healers of mankind, who usually stride down the corridors in their white coats, wrapped in dignity and authority. Here they are, lying with their asses in the air, wild with the pleasure of teasing a respectable nurse.

Siv bursts out laughing. She is unable to stop herself

and completely gives up trying to prevent them from doing
what they are doing.

She sits down on the floor beside them, tears running
down her cheeks. How idiotic this all is! What fun it all is!

Suddenly there is someone standing in the door. It is
Auntie.

"Okay, what's going on here?"

The three jump to their feet, stand looking at her as if
it is beyond them as to how she can stand there with her
hands on her hips and dark thunderclouds in her eyes.

"Aren't you ashamed of yourselves!"

This is said with such pathos, with such an exaggerated
amount of disgust, that, God help them, they burst out
laughing again.

Siv collects all her strength, straightens up and says
with a husky, tear-drowned voice, "I really must beg your
pardon. We have behaved dreadfully, and I'm very sorry."

But really! How can an apology be convincing when
you are standing there crying with laughter?

Siv struggles wildly to be serious and is finally successful.

Then her brave exertions are destroyed.

One of the interns puts an arm on Siv's shoulder, and
with great, deeply felt heroism says, "She's innocent!"

She breaks down again and stutters in despair, "I
couldn't h-h-help laughing. They are so funny."

"They are drunk."

But something is about to happen. Auntie's face is no
longer stern: All her wrinkles are disappearing.

The three sinners stand there looking at her, stiff with
surprise and relief: Is she actually laughing?

And Siv says ecstatically, "Then you're not angry?"

They hear Auntie make some strange, half-smothered
sounds. "You rascals! Imagine dropping flowers on the head
of an old nurse!"

The four of them look at each other, shaking their heads
with relief.

Then Auntie raises a finger in warning. "But it's best
you fellows go home. No more foolishness tonight."

And she trips away with her cap merrily bouncing on
her gray, understanding knot of hair.

A final giggle, the interns leave, and the night is again
quiet.

CHAPTER FOURTEEN

There are caps of foam on the breakwater.

The wild waves lash at the seaweed-covered stones with a foaming anger. Siv stands by the tar-covered railing. Her long hair has a touch of storm and sea. She lifts her face and bathes it in the dense mist of salt water.

She loves this magnificent, violent sea!

She stands there so long that the icy wind makes her cold and giddy. She feels the cold penetrate her raincoat and walks home with hasty steps.

Svend sits in her room, waiting. She has given him a key so that he can let himself in, and, to tell the truth, it is really necessary.

Because she is never there at the appointed time.

He is irritated. He can never count on her. Never! She should at least have had enough upbringing in her life so that she could be at home when she knows that he is coming.

She is, of course, out taking one of her customary walks.

Nobody wants to be out in such weather, nobody except this silly girl who never finds the cold unpleasant, and who loves snow, storms and hail.

He knocks his pipe against the stupid, little feminine ashtray, empties it, and refills it. Yes, Svend has started smoking!

Always having to wait. Always having to wait. He cannot hold out much longer if she keeps this up. He sits there becoming more and more convinced that he is a damn idiot.

But he keeps sitting.

She returns, dripping wet, wind-blown and joyously fresh. "My God, are you here already?"

"It's nine o'clock. We had agreed on eight."

"Oh, well!—But it can't be nine already?"

"It is. It *always* is. Can't you learn to watch the time?"

"I think my watch runs too fast."

"I happen to know that it doesn't."

He sits there, injured, sour, sucking on his pipe, angry and irritated.

She takes off her raincoat, throwing it carelessly over the washbasin.

It is too wet to hang up in the closet.

She dries her hair with a Turkish towel so that it stands up in untidy profusion around her pale, dark face. Then she looks at Svend. It is unbelievable how sinister a man can look when he sits sucking on a pipe.

"Are you still angry?"

As a matter of fact, he is not. He pulls himself together, smiles. Can't she understand that he thinks it strange that she does not show more interest in his visits, that she is late almost every time?

Siv is aware of all this, but she does not *want* to think too hard about why she completely forgets Svend when she is out for a walk, rummaging around in her own thoughts. She does not want to think about how unkind she is to him, how she rules and commands, so that the poor fellow is confused and unsure.

Because she cannot change the way things are.

She sits down across from him. "Do you know what I bought today?"

"No, how should I know? But I'm sure it's something you shouldn't have."

"A big chicken."

"Oh."

"I want to eat it now."

"Now?"

"Yes, it has to be fried first, of course. I'll go out and put it on the stove, and you can have half of it if you'll stop sulking."

"Don't you get enough to eat in the hospital's canteen?"

"I get so tired of all that steamed food. It all tastes the same."

"You can't afford anything else."

"No, but I'm hungry!"

She gets up, ruffles his hair as she walks past him. "Can't you be a little bit nice now!"

The chicken is frying in the kitchen. Peace has again been established in the warm little nurse's room.

Svend sits looking thoughtfully at her, really wanting to understand her. "Can't you explain to me why you're always out taking walks? The weather was terrible this evening."

She looks nervously at him, at his clean, vulnerable, masculine head, feeling the offended and strained noble manliness which shines from his being and stature. What can she say? She cannot explain it to him. They have never been able to talk about such things.

"Shall I tell him about the boy, a drunken waiter, sixteen years old, who yelled for his mother who never came? Who told me that he loved me and coughed up blood all over my naked arms?

"Or about the woman who gave birth to a lively baby boy while she lay unconscious from sleeping pills. She was a prostitute.

"I could also tell him about the soldier who was unable to hide his desire when I washed his lower parts, or about the funny fellow in room fifteen who made the ward nurse angry. She came into his room asking for me, and he pulled back his blanket and said that he'd see if I was there.

"There's also Old Thomas, who cries if he isn't pushed out into the hall during the dinner break, so that he can have his after-dinner cigar. There is also that idiot who goes to the toilet with a blanket wrapped around his stomach, rips it down the middle and wipes himself with one half, which he later carefully shoves down the toilet bowl.

"Could I tell Svend that I have landed in the middle of life, in the middle of all these people—and that I am fond of them all?

"All this has something to do with my walks, but it is too difficult to explain; it is too much trouble."

"Why don't you answer?"

"Well, I don't know. I just know that I need to."

The chicken is fried.

Siv comes in with the skillet, puts it on a wooden block on the table.

Svend looks at her with a worried expression. "Are we going to eat it like this?"

"Yes, isn't this good enough?"

"Well, I mean, without any bread?"

"Here's a plate for you to put your half on. I don't have any bread, and anyway, we'll never manage to eat it all."

"I only want a little piece. I don't like to eat chicken without bread. I don't want to be difficult, but it doesn't taste right this way."

Like a flash of lightning, Siv's eyes glow with anger. "Oh, you always make a muddle out of everything."

He smiles disarmingly.

Siv's anger disappears. She picks up a thigh, pulling the poor creature to pieces. "Here's a piece for you. I'll eat the rest."

"You'll never be rich."

"Oh, yes I will."

"If you marry me and keep up with these expensive habits, we'll soon be ready for the poorhouse."

Siv looks teasingly at his annoyed face. Svend is rich, or, to be more exact, his father is. He owns several textile mills, and Svend is his only heir.

She is unable to imagine how she is going to make Svend poor.

Suddenly she begins to snicker, and finally laughs aloud, gasps and almost gets food down her windpipe.

"What's the matter now?"

"Oh!" She makes a brave attempt to control herself. "Oh!"

"Yes?"

"I just happened to think that I—that at any rate I can urinate."

"You can what? Have you lost your mind?"

Seeing Svend's half-annoyed, half-suspicious face, she breaks down completely. The chicken falls to the floor.

Svend leans over, nobly, and picks it up. He gives her his handkerchief so that she can wipe her face, which is streaked with tears and chicken fat.

"Well, can I have some kind of explanation now?"

"Of course. You see, there is a patient in my ward, he's very, very rich. He has a white telephone in his room, a radio, wine and expensive flowers. He has jewels on his fingers and goes to the toilet in an expensive dressing gown of pure silk—and—"

"Yes, go on, and—?"

"Well, I stood by his bed yesterday looking at a big basket of flowers—orchids—and so I said that it must be wonderful to be so rich. But—but—he just looked sadly at me, and then he said—"

"Go on."

"He said, and don't forget how sad he looked, he said—"

"Yes?"

"Hell, little girl, what good is it being rich when you can't *piss?*"

Siv collapses completely, throws herself back in her chair. "Well I can, at any rate. I can eat chicken and—everything else."

Svend has to laugh, too. He cannot help himself.

He bends over and kisses her. "You're impossible. I can never really be angry with you. But now I've got to go home and read."

"First, you've got to tuck me in."

"Okay, but you've got to hurry up then."

Siv undresses, slowly, full of terrible, feminine sadism. She tears the bedspread off the bed, crawls comfortably in under the blanket.

"Do you mind taking out the skillet and opening the window?"

He obeys. Then he sits down on the bed. "Now I'm going to tuck you in." He sees that the blanket fits tightly around her, gives her a gentle kiss on her mouth and forehead. "Good night, my dear."

"Hummph—good night!"

The light is turned out and the door closes behind him. Weren't his eyes a little red and his voice a little strained? Well, it is probably because he reads so much. He is just—like a big brother.

And the sweet girl puts her arm behind her neck, looks into the darkness, and thinks unrefined thoughts.

CHAPTER FIFTEEN

Most of the rooms on the floor have several patients. Some have three patients, others have seven or eight in them.

But there are also one or two private rooms on the floor.

The patient who lies in a private room has the money to pay for extra care. There is always a cloth napkin placed on his tray. He is always served his food on a covered plate and is given three different dishes a day. If there is a particularly delicious dish and there is not enough for all the patients, the private patient is offered some first.

A man lying in a private room has money. He has a noteworthy position in society. Even if the head physician does not have enough time to visit all the rooms, he has to consult in the private rooms, in any case, because only the head physician is in charge of the treatment of these patients.

And there is no stiff, solemn tone in this room during his visit. The head physician sits pleasantly on the edge of the bed or in the armchair, accepts the cigarette or cigar which is offered him, speaks to the patient like one wise man to another, asking what he thinks about the progress of his treatment, whether he would like this or that, whether he might possibly consider . . . ?

The head physician and the private patient are very good friends. The blanket does not always have to be smooth—and what's this about not being allowed to smoke in the rooms? Are there really patients who are not allowed to do that? A human being just like everybody else, not being allowed to find solace in a cigarette?

No, the patient in the private room does not have such thoughts. He thinks everything is very excellent. Can there really be people who complain about the food, about the lack of human kindness? He cannot imagine them. They must be just grouches, and you find them anywhere, especially among people who lack culture.

The head nurse, Miss Knudsen, curtseys in and asks if the food tasted all right, if the mattress is comfortable, if there is anything bothering him? In dismay she discovers that the student nurse has forgotten to remove the obligatory rubber sheet under the cotton sheet on hospital beds. How terrible! A private patient does not need a rubber sheet. It is hot and unpleasant to lie on, and he never upsets his urine bottle or soils his bed in other ways. She removes the rubber sheet, blushing with annoyance. She must find out who the presumptuous student was who forgot this.

She sits down in the armchair and appears to have a very good time. He offers her a glass of wine, man of the world that he is. She thanks him, blushes, sips at her wine and looks searchingly at the table: It needs a new tablecloth. That rag does not give a very good impression of the hospital.

She sweats under her arms from pleasure, nods and chats. It is so wonderful that there are also patients you can *talk* to.

It happens that in the other rooms there are patients who cannot be cured. They grimace because of doors which are constantly slamming open or closed. They are fed gruel by an impatient student nurse who cannot get through fast enough.

But that is how things are.

A new patient has been placed in the private room!

The armchair has been taken out into the bath and has been washed with a stiff brush. Clean curtains have been hung, and there are three pillows on the bed instead of the usual two. The floor is washed and polished. Everything has been prepared in the best possible way. Clothes hangers are hanging in the closet, good suit hangers so that the trousers do not have to be hung on nails. There are ashtrays in the room and a thin water glass on the night table.

Siv had not met the patient. He was driven up and moved immediately into his room.

A private patient does not have to be bathed before he enters the hospital bed.

You know very well that people with money always wash themselves before they leave home.

A new entry in the book on the desk. Siv peeks in it with curiosity. "Private room!" This is written at the top of the page in capital letters. And underneath: "Heinz Gertsen, antique dealer."

The diagnosis is a slipped disc. Yes, that can be painful.

Heinz Gertsen? She has not heard of him, has she? Oh, yes, he is supposed to be some sort of fox—and loaded with money!

A colleague comes in and also reads. She nudges Siv. "Have you heard about him?"

"Yes. A little."

"He's a wolf, you know."

They turn quickly to the other side of the page. There is very little written about him, but he is married and has two children.

Siv turns to her colleague. "Have you been in there?"

"Yes." She nods and laughs. She is Polish. A small, solid girl with a round, smiling face.

"He's dangerous."

"What do you mean by 'dangerous'?"

Her colleague grabs her hips and twists herself in front of Siv. "Very dangerous for small, innocent girls."

Siv absolutely has to see this man!

She walks into the kitchen and finds a glass, fills it with ice water, puts on her most professional air and bustles down to the end of the corridor, hesitating outside the private room, which has double, soundproof doors.

Then she tosses her head back, looks superior and shoves open the doors with her elbow.

She looks quickly at the bed, puts the tray down on a table and approaches, stretching out her hand. "Good day, my name is Siv Esruth."

She sings out her name with a husky, embarrassed voice, lets her eyes wander over the blanket and a pair of large, white hands, lets them follow the body in the blue-striped pajamas until she encounters the man's face.

He has taken her hand, pressing it warmly and linger-ingly. She looks into a couple of blue-gray, narrow, smiling eyes, sees a pale, beautiful face, a large, sensual mouth with gold glittering among the teeth, sees a smile, a fatherly, curious and tired smile.

His hair is blond and brushed back from his high temples, his nose is long and straight, with thin, vibrating nostrils, and his narrow, smiling eyes are a little on an angle. This gives his whole face a look of superiority.

Siv shrinks a bit. He is too grand, elegant and sure of himself. She moves her glance from his face down to his hand, which slowly lets go of hers. It is a beautiful hand. It is very large and has long, flexible fingers. On one of his fingers shines a ring with a clear, polished stone. Can it be a diamond?

She breathes deeply. Well. She cannot let him think that he has impressed her. She is as good as he is, even if she does not have money and expensive jewelry.

She has told him her name and he has told her his.

Is there anything else to say? No, at any rate Siv cannot think of anything else. She turns to put the ice water on the table (there is a glass there already). He laughs a little and grabs her apron without embarrassment.

"You are pretty young, aren't you?"

He says this slowly, as if he never says anything without having thought it over first, or as if he cannot be bothered by rushing.

She tosses her head. "I look younger than I am."

"Hmm!"

He lets her go, and she walks quickly out of the room, having made up her mind that she cannot stand him. What a conceited man! Old, and burned-out besides! How old is he?

She has a chance to read in the day book: "thirty five years old."

And he is married, rich and blasé. Just the way he looked at her, as if he knew something about her. He has probably known a lot of girls. Yes, she has heard about that.

And he is a man of standing, one of those the head physician jokes with.

He is revolting!

But she has to go into his room once again.

She has a little bucket in her hand, a dry and a wet

cloth and a bottle of alcohol. She has to wash his wash-basin. She has thrown the clean towels over her shoulder. She is not supposed to do so, because Miss Knudsen says that it does not look nice, that she looks as if she is a waitress in some third-class restaurant. But Miss Knudsen is not on duty.

Siv looks at the clock in the corridor: ten-thirty. She has plenty of time. The doctor does not begin his rounds before eleven, and the other nurses are busy cleaning up the other rooms.

Siv walks into the private room, nods, smiles, puts down her bucket and starts to work.

"What energy! Do you have to do all this?"

She nods stiffly. "Yes, sir."

"Hmm!" He always says "Hmm," and is always lying there staring at her as if she were some sort of strange animal. She glances quickly at his bed and hurriedly looks back again. She thinks his eyes are cold and glittering and very impudent.

It is also very impolite of him to look at her the whole time instead of reading the book he has lying on his blanket, especially when he looks at her like *that*.

She feels that he wants to embarrass and confuse her. He seems to enjoy the effect which his eyes have on the slender back of this girl who is polishing the mirror and the washbasin as if it had not been done for a long time. She hurries and finishes, gives him a short nod and leaves the room.

But she is also given the job of washing his basin the following day—and the next. It is a strange coincidence, isn't it? Her colleagues think so, too, and they smile a little. But they don't say a word; they just look at her with curiosity when she runs off with her bucket and cloths.

But Mr. Gertsen has no idea of this, and this comforts her. He does not know anything about the work schedule of the hospital and must think it quite normal that the same student nurse cleans his washbasin every day.

Or does he?

He looks at her as he usually does, is silent.

Siv becomes desperate. She stands by the basin, looks at herself in the mirror, sees her brown, thin face, her black, shiny eyes, her hair which falls out from under her cap and down on her forehead, her taut, white collar which encircles her straight and stubborn neck. She stands there in front of the mirror, lost in her own beauty.

"Yes, it must be a pleasure for you to look at yourself in the mirror, Miss."

The strange, silent man has said something!

She blushes: He is making fun of her!

And although she is completely in agreement with him, she turns and asks, "Why?"

"Do you really want to know? Because you are very lovely, that's why."

He laughs, takes a puff on the cigarette which is always to be found between his long, white fingers. He does not laugh loudly, resoundingly, like other good men. He laughs quietly and with a clucking sound as if he does not want to share his laughter with everyone.

Siv breathes deeply and gathers up all her courage. She wants to shock him. She wants to embarrass him. She wants to defy this man-about-town who irritates and provokes her.

She walks over to the foot of his bed, takes hold of its iron bars as though on the deck of a ship, and says, maliciously and quietly, "Why do you lie there looking at me all the time?"

"Because it's a pleasure to look at you."

He has not lost control yet. He just looks at her contentedly and with curiosity.

She flares up. Now I'll tell him. "It's impolite of you to stare at me in that way."

"In what way?" He smiles and Siv becomes furious.

"So fresh—and—and—insolent. Yes, you are fresh, you know. It's embarrassing the way you stare, and you're quite aware of the fact."

She breathes deeply, waiting for his answer.

He does not answer at once, just lies there smoking, looking at her and at the smoke which is thick because of all his cigarettes.

She triumphs: Good, at last he has been embarrassed.

Then he sits up in his bed, puts out the cigarette in the ashtray and stares more unabashedly at her than ever before.

"Come here and give me a kiss!"

She stiffens, dismayed.

He smiles as if he had only asked her to move the table or shake his pillow.

She shifts from one foot to the other, blushes, wants to tear herself away from the bed-post, disappear down the hall and let him lie there without an answer. But she stays there, feeling in her overwrought fantasy that she is standing at the gates of hell.

She looks at his mouth. It is soft and sensual, but has a cynical turn as if it had tasted something which was bitter and sour. His eyes are not warm, not tender like Svend's, but they are beautiful. They have surely seen a lot, so much that perhaps they can also see her dreams and erotic fantasies.

This is what she thinks as she stands there holding on to the foot of the bed. She whispers stupidly and in confusion, "I'm engaged."

"You don't look engaged."

That Polish girl was right: He is dangerous!

It is precisely because of this that Siv is unable to tear herself away. She must get out of his room now, she must avoid his cynical eyes, his white hands and his silent, stimulating stares which transfix her.

At last she is able to pull herself together. She turns, gropes for her bucket, does not look back at Heinz, walks over to the doors and opens them as carefully as if there were a mortally ill patient lying in the room. She disappears into the hall, with the sound of his laughing in her ears, walks into the washroom and pours out the water.

What is she to do?

She lies awake at night letting him take her in her imagination. She wants to, she does not want to! She will not go into his room to clean it up, she will not talk to him, she will not bring him his food.

But she does all this just the same!

Siv's colleagues begin to look at her with cold, curious eyes: What's going on between Mr. Gertsen and Siv? Why is she always in his room? It is not very nice of her. Hadn't she better take that ring off her finger first?

Siv knows that the others are talking about her, but she cannot help herself. In the mornings she often firmly resolves that the day before her will be different. But she still goes into his room and cleans up, she straightens up his bed and brings him his food.

The ward nurse has also noticed what is going on. But she does not say anything. Mr. Gertsen is a private patient, and imagine what would happen if Siv told him that she had reprimanded her about something? No, she will not get mixed up in the situation.

Heinz Gertsen has begun talking to Siv, more than he has ever done before. But it is *what* he says—and the way in which he says it.

He says that he will have her, that he is completely sure he will get her, that she is too pretty for her own good. And he looks at her as if she were as dissolute as *he* surely is.

But one evening Siv goes to prayer meeting again and is captured by the spirit there. Her father is absolutely right; he has always said that Satan is deceitful and foxy. You have to be on your guard or else things will turn out badly and something terrible will happen. You must not entertain sinful thoughts.

And isn't that what she has been doing? She has flirted with every man she has seen, enjoyed their eyes and their lusts, she has painted her lips and looked impertinent.

The next day, when she enters his room, she has made an important decision: She will tell him what she thinks of him. She will make him so angry that he will never speak to her again.

He looks at her in the same way he has always done. He smiles, smokes, asks her if she is Danish.

Yes, she is, but he won't find out anything else.

"I am also a religious Christian."

"You're also a *what?*" He looks surprised.

She nods stiffly. "Yes, I'm religious, and so are my parents and my fiancé. So, you see, I'm not your cup of tea."

"Hmm," he says—always this "Hmm." But his eyes become more serious.

"Is that why you think you're not my type, Siv?"

She ignores his calling her by her first name. "Yes."

Perhaps he thinks that he is good enough for a religious girl, married as he is and still having other girls. He, who is the cause of her being unable to sleep at nights, who causes her to burn things and suck in her abdomen if she just walks past his door.

He has it coming to him.

She has walked over to the door carrying her bucket and cloths. She puts the bucket down and looks angrily at him.

"Now you just listen to me, Mr. Gertsen. You are a pig. You are impudent and degenerate and I'm much too good for you. What do you want to mess around with me for? Can't you find enough girls of your own kind? And don't think that I'm impressed by the fact that you have money and are handsome, either. Because your face is ugly, ugly and cynical. I'll never have anything to do with you, never. And I must ask you to be so kind as not to call me by my first name."

Siv says all of this, and lots more.

She pours over him every mocking, disparaging thing she can think of. She charges him with the responsibility for her uneasiness and nervousness, her fear and her longing.

Heinz has sat up in bed. At first he looks at her in amazement, then his expression changes. Is it compassion, a vague understanding which is revealed in his face? Siv will not look at it, will not understand it. She continues her rampage.

Finally, he mumbles, "Well, I'll be damned!" He does not say anything else, but just keeps repeating this phrase several times. And he does not get angry. No matter what she says, she is unable to change the expression on his calm, interested face or the warm look in his gray eyes which Siv has never seen before.

She is almost unable to control herself. She wants to strike him, but then she would have to walk over to his bed, and he might grab her.

She is on the verge of bursting into tears, in anger and helplessness. She has emptied herself and has no more to say.

She opens the door. "You won't see any more of me. I'll see to it that I avoid your room."

She closes the door and pretends that she does not hear a quiet "goodbye" from the big sinner in the white sickbed.

Siv stays away from the private room for a couple of days.

Then one of her colleagues comes to her and sticks a letter in her hand—it is from Heinz. She goes into the bathroom, locks the door, sits on the edge of the bathtub and opens the letter with trembling hands.

He writes that he *must* speak with her, that he cannot stand not having her in his room. She does not have to be afraid, he won't harm her, but she *must* come; otherwise he'll make a scandal.

He also writes that he is in love with her. He writes so many nice things that she is completely overwhelmed.

And so, there she is in his room again!

She smiles somewhat embarrassed, he smiles from joy and contentment. He gives her a package.

She takes it expectantly in her hands. "What is it?"

"A peace offering."

"I won't take any presents from you."

"Well, open it up."

He sits in bed looking at her in suspense. He does not seem conceited. She gives in and opens the package. It contains a handwrought, very beautiful gold bracelet.

She breathes deeply and trembles. "I can't accept it."

"Nonsense."

"It's not nonsense, because what do you expect in return?"

He leans back in bed, takes a puff on his cigarette, not looking at her but at the wall.

"Please take it!" He says this slowly and with a friendly tone and turns his face to look at her. The blue-gray eyes are completely blue and the soft voice is new and strange to her.

She waits, looking at the beautiful bracelet, looking at the man.

She puts the bracelet down on the night table. "I'm not in love with you, and I won't fall in love with you just because you give me a bracelet. You know very well that I'm engaged and that *you* are married. The whole thing is just crazy."

"You *are* in love with me."

"But I don't *want* to be."

She is no longer so afraid of this man. Something has happened, she is not sure what it is, but something has happened. There has been a change in Heinz. She has almost become equal to him and the situation.

But he stretches out his hand, picks up the bracelet and gives it back to her. "Take it. If I get anything in return, so much the better. If I don't, you're welcome to it. A lovely girl ought to have lovely things."

"Then it doesn't matter if you don't get anything in return?"

Siv looks carefully and nervously at him.

He smiles, and says, calmly and frankly, "I'll be paid some day."

"No!" She throws the jewelry on the bed. "No!"

He picks the bracelet up again, and hands it to her once more. "Okay, as you like, but take it anyway—as a compliment."

And Siv, the vain, immoral devil she is, takes it in her hand and lets it slide up over her arm. She looks at it; she smiles; she turns, showing it off. Just the fact that Our Lord has made me so delightful—is justification enough! She has a right to this bracelet.

She looks searchingly at his face. He is not laughing at her, is he? No, he is just looking seriously at her.

She whispers her thanks and backs out through the door—with a very bad conscience and the bracelet in the pocket of her uniform.

CHAPTER SIXTEEN

The weeks that follow are exciting and wonderful.

Heinz is still in the hospital. Siv fluctuates between fear and rapture, fear and love.

She takes her Sunday walks with Svend. She goes to prayer meeting with her father and mother, but she sits through the unison singing seething with expectation of her night duty when she will see Heinz.

Most of what happens during these weeks only happens in Siv's mind—but that is quite a lot.

When she is on night duty, the bell rings from the private room.

She has to go in there to stop the bell. It continues to ring until she comes.

She stands in the door and asks, "What do you want, Mr. Gertsen?"

He looks up with a teasing smile. "I want a kiss!"

But he does not get a kiss. Siv hurries out again, nervous and annoyed. The bell rings again a little while later. This time he is hungry.

"At this time of night?"

"Yes, can't you find me something to eat?"

"Well, yes, I guess I can."

She comes back with a tray and a plate: fried potatoes, sausage and a fried egg.

He sits up in the bed, eating with a good appetite, and he finds a bottle of wine in the night table, pours them each a large glass full.

Siv has to go out and look after the other patients, but as soon as she has a little free time, she is back again in his room. She does something to his bell system so that she can hear in his room if somebody rings from another.

She transforms his room to the on-duty room, sitting with him half the night.

During the day no one can understand why Mr. Gertsen is always asleep. But the poor man must be allowed to sleep some time.

And what happens on those nights that Siv is on duty and violates all the rules by sitting in a patient's room?

He likes to have her sit on the edge of his bed so that he can reach her. He sticks his hand up under her dress until he touches the soft skin on the inside of her thigh— but then Siv pulls away, he is not allowed to go any farther, and he is not allowed to kiss her. Because then she can still say to herself and Svend with a good and calm conscience that she has never been kissed by anyone other than her fiancé.

But things happen just the same! She notices it in Heinz Gertsen and she feels it when she sits in his room, comfortably leaning back in the armchair, just talking.

Because she is able to talk with him now! She discovers that she can talk very easily with this man who is so different from her and her world. He is interested in what she says, and he makes comments in unusually reserved sentences which cause her to ask for more.

They philosophize and discuss, talk about life, religion and politics (which Siv does not understand at all). She tells him about her home. She also tells him that she is a virgin and that she will wait until she is married. She tells him about her father.

"You understand, Mr. Gertsen" (he is unable to get her to call him by his first name), "we are very fond of each other, my father and I!"

She tells him that she is a gypsy, sits arched forward in the chair, looking engagingly at him, expecting him to understand everything that she does not herself understand.

And what does Heinz say to all of this?

He tells her about Copenhagen, about the bars, about the whores whom he thinks are also human beings, and who can be much better acquaintances than other kinds of women.

He tells her about all the places he has been, about German, French and Italian girls, about Venice, where you sail in a gondola with your lover. He tells her about life and the world, about painting and literature, recommends some books for her to read.

He sits with a cigarette in his mouth, squinting because

of the smoke, while he uses both hands to paint life and the world for her.

He pours her a glass of wine.

Siv shakes her head from side to side, is slightly tipsy, even though she has only had a single glass. She still has to look after the ward on the top floor as well.

She is amazed and enchanted. Somebody like him, who knows so much about everything, is actually interested in her and her problems.

Yes, he is. Because he is in love, warm, enchanted, as you become when you have experienced something new after having thought that new things were not to be found in your life. As you become after having been convinced that everything was, as it is said in the Bible, complete emptiness.

Yes, this tall, blond man with the broad shoulders is enchanted. He lies there pouring out wine, destroying his night's sleep and worshipping a gypsy girl who is the most primitive creature God ever created!

And Siv grows—grows until she is a match for his six-foot body.

She can allow herself to be coquettish and capricious. She can say what she likes, be frank, outspoken and honest.

She can tell him about all her peculiar problems: about her bourgeois home, about her gypsy father who reads his Bible and yet can tell her, *"That's* the best thing that a cat knows."* She can tell him about the meetings in which she has stood up and talked—about the Holy Ghost. And also about what she does now and then at night.

She has never told anyone any of this! It flows out of her. She has never dared to be honest, but *now* she can because of an instinctive feeling that Heinz understands it and understands it in the *right* way.

But if he had appeared to have smiled just once because of Siv's strange explanations, if he had just once put on some sort of patronizing look when she, with clenched hands and red cheeks, had told him about Sacho? Yes, then Siv would have closed up like an oyster which can be opened neither with a hammer nor a chisel.

But Heinz is not like that—not with *her.*

He listens, he questions, he says, "My child!"

But he says it calmly and finely, without sentimentality

or condescension. He says it as if he knew the whole thing before she had begun to tell it to him.

He wants to see her in her own clothes. She puts on her prettiest dress, brushes her hair so that it falls, shiny and thick, about her face and sneaks in to him one evening when she is free.

And he sits up in his bed so that he can reach the bed-post at the foot of the bed with his long hands—and says everything that she had expected to hear.

But Siv becomes a little reflective when she encounters a glance in his small, gray eyes which is too warm. When she sees that his mouth has completely lost its cynical, bitter expression which she encountered the first day she saw him.

She is not going to do anything for him—not what he wants her to do. It is just that it is so nice to *talk* to him.

She does not love him. They belong to different worlds, and he is married. Siv has seen his wife. She resembles Siv, even though she is older. A dark, long-haired girl in slacks. Siv saw her as she came swishing down the hall on the way to the toilet.

Mr. Gertsen's room is located at the end of a long corridor where the building turns sharply. When you stand in the room at the opposite end of the building, you can see into his windows.

One day, while his wife is visiting him, Siv is in this room opposite his. She can see that the curtains have been closed.

A colleague, who is helping her with a sick patient, whispers and laughs, "Look, the curtains are drawn. They're probably sitting in there kissing each other, you know, as if they'll stop at *that*."

Siv's body becomes stiff with unrest. Can it be true? Yes, but, then, they have a right to. They are married, aren't they? Yes, but if he loves his wife *that* much—how then can he be in love with Siv?

It is really disgusting to think about and impossible to understand.

When she goes into his room later with his evening meal, she looks at him with an aloof, dignified expression. She carefully puts the tray on the table, finds his napkin with a professional air and says nothing.

He looks at her with surprise. "Well, what've I done *now?*"

"Nothing."

He seizes her hand before she can move away from the bed. "Oh, yes there is. What's wrong?"

She straightens up, looking warmly at him. "You haven't done anything which you haven't a perfect right to do, but I saw you kiss Mrs. Gertsen. I could see you from that room over there opposite yours. You have a right to —I—I just don't trust you any more."

She stares at his face in desperation, but he just looks surprised—and then annoyed—and then happy.

"It's not true, so you can't have seen it, but you are jealous though, aren't you?"

She blushes and gets angry with herself. What a fool she has made of herself.

She rushes out of the room, and he watches her go with eyes that do not have a trace of shame in them.

It is seven o'clock and time to say good night to the patients. You open and close doors, singing out a pleasant "Good night" to all the beds. Now you can all relax, you're by yourselves now, your own masters!

Siv walks up to the private room. It is not necessary that she say good night to Heinz. No one would think it strange if she didn't, would they?

She stands a while considering—but walks into his room just the same.

"Good night!"

She seems unwilling.

He waves to her beseechingly. "Well, come on in, you crazy creature, and wish me a nice 'good night.' "

The corners of Siv's mouth tighten. She is already pacified.

He gives her a box of chocolates. "For you!"

"No, thank you."

"You can come get it later if you like. I'll be in the entire evening, you know."

He smiles somewhat bitterly and she closes the door again.

That evening she goes to a birthday party for one of her friends. They are given cocktails. Siv does not know what is in the cocktails. She has no idea about such things, but they taste good and she drinks several glasses.

She leaves the party in a light-headed and blissful state of intoxication. She does not just want to go back up to her room, undress and go to bed and sleep. Didn't Heinz have a box of chocolates for her?

Oh, how this man sits in her mind like a jack-in-the-box. She only has to open the top a little bit and all sorts of thoughts and desires stream out. He's probably asleep? But she only wants the chocolates, and she can take them even if he is sleeping, can't she? But what if he isn't asleep? Well, she only came for the chocolates, didn't she?

She sneaks up the stairs. Luckily she does not have to cross the corridor to get to his room, which is right opposite from the head of the stairs. Carefully—oh, so carefully—she opens the doors, first one, then the other. She closes them behind her and sneaks over to his bed. He's asleep, lying on his back and looking innocent.

The box of chocolates is on the table on the other side of the bed. Can she go around the bed to get it?

No! She stands there quite silently in the faint light, looking at the sleeping man. Can he really be asleep? She thinks she notices a slight movement of his eyelids. What if he isn't really asleep? Then if she bends over the bed to reach the chocolates, he can rise up at once and kiss her, can't he? He'll believe that he has surprised her, and that is not at all what she wants to happen.

All this rushes through Siv's brain in the course of a few seconds. She bends over the bed, slowly, stretches out her arm—and knows that what she wants to happen will happen.

He rises up quickly. She is completely enclosed in his arms for the first time.

She becomes stiff and difficult, gasps and resists, becomes soft and permissive. He kisses her, crushes her against him and kisses her with his lips, his tongue and teeth, laughing with joy and triumph.

She carefully puts her arm around his neck, bores her hands into his neck and drowns in his kisses and caresses.

Finally he lets go of her.

She stands up and straightens her hair, strokes herself along her body, trembling and exhausted. Will this happen again? No, it won't. Heinz is the captain of this ship of love, and he will not take her in a hospital bed. She lays a trembling hand on the door. She must go now. She has sobered up and has remembered that the night nurse could possibly come in on her fast rounds.

There has been silence between them, but Heinz then says quietly, "Thank you." He is sitting in his bed, his smooth, blonde hair is unkempt, standing up in stiff locks from his high forehead. He does not look elegant and aristocratic. He looks happy and whispers, "Thank you, thanks."

He repeats it over and over with a sort of thrill in his voice that makes Siv get a lump in her throat. My Lord, was it *that* good?

He makes her feel that she is a goddess who has bestowed a favor on a poor sinner.

She stands there, shaking, trembling and amazed.

But she does not know what to say to him in return. Therefore, she just smiles, waves to him and hurries out.

She goes to her room and crawls under her blanket, laying her hand firmly on the soft, wooly handful between her thighs. He had thanked her—and he had actually *meant* it, hadn't he?

Isn't it possible that God—in spite of everything—understands all this?

CHAPTER SEVENTEEN

One day Heinz begs her, imploringly and suggestively, "Stand over by the wall, Siv, and unbutton your dress. I know you don't have much on underneath. No one will come in at this time of day. Let me see you without your clothes on."

"No!" Siv shakes her head with determination. "No, no!"

Somebody could come in. Just think if they did while she stood in a hospital room displaying herself.

"Do you have any photographs of yourself—without clothes on?"

She laughs. "Yes, when I was a baby."

Now go over against the wall and take off your clothes. I won't touch you. I only want to look at you."

"Not for the world."

It is very annoying that she has no such picture. She would not mind showing him her loveliness—but how?

Now that she thinks of it, Svend has a camera.

A few days later she takes a walk with Svend in the woods.

They have the camera with them. Siv has asked him to bring it along. "We're going to take pictures of each other today, aren't we, Svend?"

Of course, if she would like to, then so would he.

He walks swinging her hand back and forth. "Just think, Siv, in a few months you'll no longer be a student nurse. I'll also have finished, and we can get married."

She nods, walking, kicking the leaves.

"We've been engaged a long time, you know."

"Yes."

Is she going to marry soon? Yes, of course she is. The time of waiting will soon be over.

But is she going to marry Svend?

Heinz—he is married, but there are many other men in the world who are not. She walks on with a strange thought: I am in love with them all—all men—with the exception of the one I am to marry.

She cannot stand it much longer. The whole thing is wrong.

"Svend, I'm in love with somebody else."

He looks at her aghast. "What did you say?"

"You heard me."

"Yes."

She looks at him from the sides of her eyes. He walks, looking down at the ground. He won't believe anything, anything about what kind of person Siv is. He only wants to know how she ought to be.

Annoyance grows and grows in Siv. It turns into an evil, uncontrollable defiance.

This evil has grown in her slowly throughout all those years of waiting. Why isn't he like other men? Why doesn't he ever know what to do with his hands?

Every now and then he puts them behind his back. It looks so ridiculous. She says sweetly and tremblingly, "You look so foolish walking with your hands behind your back."

He looks at her, hurt. "What's wrong with that? What else am I to do with them?"

"You could put them in your pockets."

He snorts, unsure. "Would that be any better?"

But the next time he meets Siv, he sticks one of his hands in his pants' pocket, smiling awkwardly and nervously. No, it looks so idiotic. She is a little sorry for him, too. He wants so much to please her. He straightens up, looks fresh and sporty, takes a firm and masculine hold of her hand, fighting his way through his inferiority complex.

Siv turns around. He looks like a fool.

She is evil and she admits this to herself. But she continues to govern and command. A few times she awakens his self-assertion. He tightens his mouth (My God, he doesn't look nice then, either. His mouth is not suited to determination). But he is actually irritated.

"You always have so much to find wrong with me that

soon I won't know how I'm to act in order to please you."

"You only have to be yourself."

She says it with surprise, consciously hurt. She hangs her head, so that he has to feel sorry for her because *he* is angry.

Svend walks on a while, looking grim. Just the same he will not give in so soon.

But she knows that he will come to do so. She expects him to put out his hand to establish peace. She waits, coldly and angrily evil. The least you can expect is that he be humble, isn't it?

Svend has some idea as to what is the matter, but he cannot change things. Especially not now, even if he went against his morals and inhibitions. Because *Siv won't*—he is not permitted to touch her, is almost not allowed to kiss her and never allowed to talk about love. She does not say so, but she shows it with her whole body, and he trembles nervously when he meets her hard, brown eyes and her strange coldness.

You young, frightened man!

Forget tenderness for a short time, and listen to that song which lies muted and forgotten beneath the cloak of civilization. Answer her harassing mocking with an explosive beating, with a hard, sure whipping. Collect your courage so that you can understand your girl and her need for strength. Afterwards, you can hold her, softly, with gentle hands.

Don't you understand? Don't you know? Don't you dare to find out? That a woman wants things that way?

Forget your father and mother. Forget your God and your educated being, and be—for a while—what you *are*.

You will never make a mistake with a woman if you learn this.

You will be a king. You will be a sheik. You will be Caruso, Cary Grant and Marlon Brando. You will be greater than the greatest hero—you will be a *man*. For you will then have discovered woman's mystery!

Then remember tenderness.

Svend asks, struggling, "You say that you have fallen in love with somebody else. Who is it?"

"A married man, so nothing can come of it. But things

can't go on this way between us if I've fallen in love with somebody else."

"Who is it?"

"Heinz Gertsen."

"The antique dealer?"

"Yes."

Svend is genuinely terrified. "Where did you meet him?"

"He's on my floor."

The woods are silent for a moment. Then Svend asks with difficulty, "Are you in love with him—do you really love him?"

"I'm not sure, but I'm crazy about him."

"Crazy about him." Svend frowns. "You talk like a stupid, superficial teenager."

"Perhaps that's just what I am."

"No, you're not." He turns excitedly toward her and grabs her shoulder. "No, you're not, because I know you."

She shakes his hand off her shoulder. "If there is anybody who does not know me, it's you."

He makes his voice stern and superior. "I've known you since you were fifteen years old."

"That's what you think." She says it so bitterly, so hard and full of mockery that he feels a nervous shock go through him.

He does not answer at once. This is very serious. This must be thought out. At last he sighs deeply, pulls her down on a tree stump and turns her toward him. "Siv, be careful!"

She asks with irritation, *"What* am I to be careful about?"

"You know what, Siv. You know very well. If you let me go, he will have you—and what then? He is married. He'll just play around with you, and you can be ruined both in body and soul."

Siv does not believe all this. It does not frighten her. Ruined in body and soul if she loses her virginity?

She is about to get furious again when Svend says, "What about your father? What do you think he'll say?"

Siv starts. Now, when she was just about to be strong —but her father? That Sacho's daughter should become a sinner!

No, she cannot bring herself to be that. But what, then? She does not know.

Svend sees her insecurity and gathers new courage. He pulls her to him and gently strokes her hair. Siv has tears on her cheeks. That is a good sign.

He tells her of his love for her. He wants to help her. Together they will resist the devil's crafty plot.

And Siv gives in. "Let us try again, then."

But nothing on earth can be so selfish, so deadly for truth, so crushing and suffocating for all good feelings than another person's sticky, demanding love.

Siv jumps up, renewed and purified, brushes away the remaining tears from her cheeks, smiles engagingly and kindly at Svend. "I thought we were going to take pictures."

"Yes." He nods heartily, wanting so badly to make her happy again. "I understand that other men can fall in love with you, because, my God, you're so sweet."

She walks trustingly close up to him. The whole thing is to start all over again. He really must believe *that*. It is a reformed little girl who stands before him.

She looks sheepishly down at the ground, scraping it with her foot. "Do you want to take a picture of me?"

"Yes I do!"

"How do you want to take it?"

"That's for you to decide."

"Would you like to have a picture of me naked?"

He blushes, glances at her and looks away. "Of course."

"Then stay here." She points to the tree stump which stands between the sun and the branches rich with leaves.

She turns around and looks questioningly at him, waves confidently to him. This good mood has to be maintained, the touching, relieved expression on Svend's face must be maintained.

She quickly undresses and sits down under the tree in the position of a mermaid.

Svend sits looking through his viewfinder, adjusts and finds the correct distance. He looks over the camera at Siv and lets his hands fall. "How sweet you are."

She frowns impatiently. "Hurry up and take the picture, before somebody comes."

He strains his strength to the utmost, gathering together again all his morality and all his good pious thoughts, puts the viewfinder in front of his eyes and takes the picture.

Afterwards, he comes close to her, trembling, moved, and sits down close beside her with his head at an angle. "How sweet you are."

Siv arches her body like a nervous cat, and she thinks desperately: "Don't touch me—not *you*—not *you*. You have no right to come any closer, no closer . . . but you can be used to take pictures."

And she will surely be able to get this picture away from him. It is really hers, since it shows her completely naked. Of course, she will get it. She will pretend that she has a bad conscience, bend her head and sadly tell him that she is sorry that she let herself be photographed like that. He will give it to her so that she can destroy this light-minded thing which was to seal their reconciliation.

But she will not burn it. No, she will have it enlarged, with a secret glance at the man in the photo store. Perhaps she will also have it tinted. And she will hide it in a drawer, show it to Heinz—and perhaps to others as well.

What a woman!

Young man, do you understand now that you need all your strength?

CHAPTER EIGHTEEN

Siv is transferred to another ward.

She says nothing to Heinz. She says good night to him, waves her hand and disappears.

What else should she have done? If she told him that she was to be transferred, he would ask for the name of the new ward and ask her to visit him. He would keep after her. And he would have his way.

She flees with herself and her confusion. She will not be able to manage this. But Heinz pursues her.

He asks her sister nurses where she is and finds out where she has been transferred. He becomes desperate. She shall not be allowed to disappear from his life in this way. Where is she now? What is she thinking about now? He will teach her to think, teach her to live. He will teach her what love is, show her what she is. And the most important thing of all: He cannot do without her. He *won't* do without her.

He gets himself released from the hospital. He will be healthy now. He has to get out and enjoy the remainder of his life, consume it, just as he has consumed so many other things.

He has become young once more—and alive.

He puts on his best clothes, fixes his hair, straightens his tie—and speculates: What does she need? She is much too thin, and she has no fountain pen. She has borrowed his numerous times.

He goes out and buys cans of shrimp, lobster, herring, mushrooms, asparagus, olives, turtle, snails, caviar. He buys crackers, cheese crackers and dessert wafers. He buys cognac, madeira, rum and cheese in bright tinfoil. He also buys a fountain pen, the best that can be found.

He then walks up to the hospital, puffing and groaning, not at all well. He asks the nurse on duty and finds out where Siv is. He goes up to her floor, but she disappears into a room and will not speak to him.

He finds out the number of her room. Later he stands otuside her door and knocks. She will not open up simply because she does not dare. He knocks again, threatens, curses, prays. At last he goes to the girl on duty, shows her the package, smiles and uses all his charm. "He *must* borrow her keys. He *must* be let into number two hundred and six."

The girl on duty is impressed: Of course, he can have the key, a splendid man like *him!* Heinz lets himself in. Siv is nervous and impressed: What more does he want of her? It's not her fault, that he dares to come in.

He puts the package down on the table, looks smilingly at her and tries to hide a tired groan. His clothes hang loosely on him. He has lost weight in the hospital. His face is pale, and pearls of sweat are on his forehead—but he smiles. He *will* be the great seducer.

Deep in her complicated female soul she becomes soft and warm because of all of this. She has been rushing toward rape and strength her whole life. And now a man is standing in front of her with loosely hanging clothes over a body that is too tall, a thin body, with pained drops of sweat on his forehead—enthusiastic and infatuated —and he *will* be a man.

She takes two steps and holds out her arms, snuggles up to him and gives him his reward. She gets hers in the sobbing sigh which comes from the big, insecure, tired man-of-the-world, from the soft receptive lips which worship hers. "So I've found you, you bad child."

He is happy now, no longer tired. Siv is aware of this and can now allow herself to be stiff and stubborn. "This was not a nice thing for you to do. I left without saying goodbye because I didn't want to have anything else to do with you. This *has* to end."

"This will never end."

He says it heavily and with assurance.

Siv trembles.

And it never does end, never really ends between Heinz and her. Not as long as one of them is alive.

She frees herself from his embrace and walks over to the table. "What's in the package?"

"Just a few things for you. You can open it later."

He sits down on the divan, she in the armchair. He offers her a cigarette. They smoke in silence. Then he says with a smile, "Aren't you glad to see me?"

"Well . . . yes."

He sits for the remainder of the time without touching her, and leaves her with a light pat on her cheek.

A strange man?

He sends her large bouquets of dark-red roses. He makes her feel like an unattainable, captivating woman.

Siv is confused: She wants to, she doesn't want to.

Is she really unattainable? Does he really think so?

He comes every day when she has free time. They talk together and he kisses and caresses her, a little more daringly, a little more violently each time they meet. But he has not yet given Siv any reason to say no. He does not let it go that far. He lets her keep her very limited ounce of virtue.

He stands there, one day, holding her in his arms, stroking her body and suddenly lifts her up and lays her right across the table with his body on hers. Quickly he removes her small, light silk panties. (Why is a woman always so easy to get to? Of course, you are supposed to scream and resist, but it would be better if the man couldn't get to you so quickly.)

It happens so quickly, and he holds her tightly.

She feels his mouth against her abdomen.

He kisses her—down there—*there!* No, *this* is awful, completely awful!

But, oh, how pleasant, how painfully, wonderfully pleasant.

She gasps, resists. It is of no use—and it feels too good, much, much too good.

But why does he like it? Is this what you call a pervert? Her friends were right. He *is* a terrible person.

"Don't do that. Don't do that!"

He does not hear her.

Siv's resistance is transformed into a quiet, joyful sob. Oh, how good it feels!

She stretches out her fingers and grabs his hair between her fingers.

He helps her down from the table and smiles at her. "Was it awful?"

She nods energetically. "Yes."

He laughs quietly. "You're the most hardened liar I've ever met."

Then he leaves.

And Siv is left alone with her new discovery: She likes such things.

Such things that are so shameful and indecent that you always have to keep them like great secrets.

Now that she thinks of it, why had Heinz been so sure that she liked it? Had he done such things to other girls, too?

Then there must be other women who like it.

But the other thing, the real thing, what about that?

When all this—when petting and kissing could be so wonderful—then that had to be—if you did it all together—that had to be completely marvelous!

A few days later she is lying by the sea.

With warm sand between her toes, with the sun's warm caress on her half-naked body and with her back buried in the wonderful, immense blue of the sea.

She stretches her body and feels herself to be healthy, healthy and young, all the way down to her soul.

And she makes a decision: She won't wait any longer. She will let Heinz teach her everything.

She has slowly wandered toward a great decision, it has slowly matured in her mind and has forced a path through all of her confusion.

And suddenly: *Now* the decision is made!

Even if all the people in the world shook their heads in warning, yelled, explained, they could not change anything.

Whenever the girl Siv makes one of her deadly serious, calm decisions, then heaven and hell can burst into pieces.

Because it is a decision she has made *with herself!*

Therefore it is unchangeable.

One day—perhaps tomorrow, perhaps in a week—Heinz will get her, anyway. She knows this as surely as she knows that the sun rises in the east and goes down in the west. She knows it with every nerve in her expectant body and with every thought in her curious mind.

It is like a rushing flood: It runs through the valley, pushing stones, gravel and logs along, rushing onward, always onward.

What good is it for a little human being to stand at its edge with hands stretched out imploringly? It won't stop for all that!

So Heinz can just as well have her *today!*

She runs out into the water and swims far out. She lies on her back, looking up at the sun and the moving clouds, and thinks calmly: "Yes, I'll do it now. I'll do it now. It has to happen, anyhow. I can think about it later, cry about it later."

She runs out of the water, dries herself quickly and puts on her clothes. Away through the woods on her bicycle.

She can get a glimpse of the yellow house through the trees. *There* it is, peaceful and well-kept, and does not know *her* at all. She stands by the telephone booth and thinks things over thoroughly: She has to ring Svend first to tell him that she won't be home in the evening. She cannot meet him right afterwards—after what's going to happen with Heinz.

She gets him on the line and tells him that she has promised to take over for a sister nurse.

Svend wishes her a pleasant time.

Then she has to ring Heinz. She searches nervously through her pockets: Does she have enough coins? Oh, yes, here they are.

She says half aloud: "Yes, now my innocence is disappearing down this little hole, first half—and then all of it."

And she puts the coins into the telephone and dials.

"Heinz. This is Siv."

"Really! *You* are calling me! What a surprise and how nice."

"Yes. I just wanted to ask—just wanted to say—that I have something for you."

Heinz's voice is calm but tense. "You have something for me?"

"Yes, if you've time to come over."

"I'll be right over."

"No, not right now. In about a half an hour. I'm not home now."

"What is it?"

She answers softly, "Just a gift!" And quickly puts down the receiver.

When she gets home, she stands quietly inside her door, looking around her room, looking at the bed, looking at the mirror.

She bends over in front of the mirror and looks searchingly into her eyes: Some say that you can tell from a girl's eyes whether she is virgin or not.

She will look at them now—and afterwards.

She slowly begins to undress. Her body beats in tense expectation, from shameful curiosity.

A wild, lamenting sound sits in her throat and will cause her to cry if she does not watch herself. But she must not cry now. She wants to be beautiful when Heinz comes.

She was so brave a moment ago—and now?

She does not answer the knocking at the door, but crawls far in under her blanket. Heinz lets himself in, walks over to the bed and looks down at a little, black head which has brown, nervous eyes.

He walks back, locks the door and sits down on the bed.

"My child, is *this* the gift you have for me?"

Siv's shame and fear fly away as if they had never existed: There is nothing here to be ashamed about. He knows how it is to be done. And he is wise and will see that she will not end up with a child. She puts all responsibility on him, stretches out her hand and bores it into his. "Yes, yes."

He puts his hands around the blanket and lifts both it and Siv up into his arms.

"What a lovely gift. A little naked girl wrapped up in a big blanket."

And everything happens, happens as it should and is good. He makes her nerves sing, so that they blot out the red pain when he enters her.

She puts her legs tightly up around his back, locks her feet and presses herself close into his large, gentle body.

He looks attentively at her, following every single movement of her strained face.

"Does it hurt? Do you want me to get off?"

She clings to him. "No, no. It feels so good and you aren't to think so much about *me*."

And she feels a togetherness, a perfect sensation of health and truth in this first embrace.

In this way I am made into a complete, true person.

She strokes his cheeks with her hands. What is it that people say about this man? That he is cynical and degenerate?

Never—never!

In this moment she loves him.

Afterwards, he sits silently in the armchair looking at her.

Siv lies well hidden under the blanket and meets his glance with pleasure.

She feels fine, but why does he look so serious, she wonders.

She asks with expectation, "Was I good?"

He grunts with a smile, "You were much too good."

After a while he says, "One would never have thought that you were a virgin."

She laughs. "Well, I'm not, you know."

"No, but you *were*."

"Yes, I was."

"I know."

He smokes carefully, drawing on the cigarette as if it were to be the last puff he will ever have in this life. And he looks so damn serious again.

Siv becomes serious. She looks thoughtfully at him. She is happy and relieved, does not quite understand, but she guesses.

So she rises up on her elbow and smiles reassuringly to him.

"To hell with that little piece of skin!"

He laughs a little strangely, goes over to her and sits down on the edge of the bed. He takes her breasts between his hands. "Yes, to hell with that little piece of skin. You little devil, you're much worse than I am."

Siv strokes his neck, laughing. "No, I can't possibly be."

He puts his hand on her sex. "Are you sore?"

"Ye—s. A little."

Then he stands up. "I've got to go now, but you'll see me soon."

He puts on his jacket, sends her a long, troubled look: Now he will go back to his business, back to his wife and children. Away from this girl he thinks is his and whom he will look after and keep, even though he knows that he does not have the least right to do so.

CHAPTER NINETEEN

Do you know what it is like to wake up in the morning of a new day which you almost dare not face? When everything that happened before the previous day has been changed and has to be seen in a new light? When everything you believed was truth has become lies and deception?

If you do, then you are a person who is on the way towards *truth!*

This is how Siv awakens.

Svend has to be told about this.

He comes in the evening, and they go for a walk.

It is a quiet, light summer evening. Siv sits down by the edge of the path and pulls at the grass.

"Svend, I've gone to bed with Heinz."

He turns toward her, surprised and disbelieving. He bends over to see her face: You can never be sure about this girl. It could just be something she said to tease him, couldn't it?

"That's not true, Siv, is it?"

"Yes, it is." She says this hard-voiced and with determination. He *has* to believe her.

He blushes from dismay and anger, stands up, clenches his fist in his pants pocket and wanders restlessly up and down by the edge of the path.

She peeks up at him. Ugh, what a muddle he is in. What is he thinking?

He stops in front of her. "Why did you do it, Siv?"

She is still seated, plucking grass, but she watches his every move.

"Well, *you* wouldn't!"

Then he explodes! He stands in front of her, so angry that tears fill his eyes and spit runs from the corners of his mouth.

"So this is the thanks I get for having controlled myself?" (Yes!)

"For not hurting you!"

(Hurting me?)

"You really are a bitch. Beginning with a married man, hell! And on top of that, such an old, worn-out cynic like Gertsen. You make me sick!"

(Nonsense.)

"If you don't watch yourself, you're going to end up as a whore. This is how they get started, you know."

Siv holds her hand in front of her mouth in order to hide her laughing lips.

He continues, but the explosion is over. There are only a few violent puffs left. "And you admit the whole thing in a tone of voice you would use if you had said: 'I've been to the hair dresser's!' But the next move is mine. I'll show you."

He walks closer to her and looks searchingly at her. "Are you laughing at me?"

"Yes, if you could just see yourself."

He walks right up to her, his eyes flushed with red.

She stands up quickly and rushes between the trees, Svend following her.

A wild, breathless, ridiculous chase which ends as Siv stumbles over a tree stump.

She saved herself!

She lies on the ground, whining, "Oh, my foot!"

He nears her, angry and suspicious. "What's wrong with you?"

She turns, "Oh, I've really twisted my foot this time!"

The poor man is sympathetic at once. "Does it hurt badly?"

"Yes."

He sits down on a tree stump and looks at her resignedly: Just as he had made up his mind!

But you cannot rape a girl who lies before you writhing in pain, can you? Especially if you have never attempted it before?

He follows her back to the hospital, and they separate outside the gate with a silent good night.

A storm rages the entire night inside Siv.

She has to go home and tell her father and mother about this, also. But how?

Should she go home and tell them tomorrow evening when she is through with her work? Yes, she had better do that. That is the most correct way of doing it, and also the best.

But if she could only find another solution. Well, they love her, don't they? But they have to find out, because she cannot stand keeping up the pretense. She is no longer afraid of Sacho's God. She does not believe in Him! There must have been a great misunderstanding some place or another. She experienced only delight, a wonderful delight when she was together with Heinz.

What a lot of rubbish all that talk about being "pure" only when you are a virgin. She cannot feel any difference. Her body is the same as it has always been, isn't it? She is sure of that *now*. Heinz also knew it: She has never been a virgin, not really. How do other women feel when they have lost their virginity? Now she is aware of the fact that she has never been virtuous. *That* must be the difference.

Siv has been converted. She has discovered a new god. This god is hers. He whispers to her that since she is what she is, it is right for her to be that way. She has not made this god by herself. She has not acquired him in order to ease a bad conscience, because she does not have a bad conscience.

She has become good friends *with herself!*

The following day she rings Svend.

"You are not to come over this evening. I want to have a little time to think the whole thing over, and you are not to say anything to my father and mother. I want to go home and tell them myself."

He answers her heavily, and with reservation, promises not to say anything and hangs up.

Then she rings up Heinz. "You can come over this evening, if you want to. I'll be alone."

He comes a few hours later when he knows that she is off duty.

He kisses her and pushes her down into a chair. "You are off tomorrow, aren't you?"

"Yes."

"I've an idea. I'll take tomorrow off. Let's drive somewhere tonight."

"Where?"

"Somewhere we can spend the night in peace."

Siv looks nervously at him. "Can we?"

"Yes, of course. I'll arrange it."

"But—shouldn't I go home first and tell everything?"

"No, you can do that afterwards."

He bends over and hides her small hands in his. They disappear completely.

"Come on. Say yes. Don't you want to do it?"

She nods. "Yes!"

She laughs joyfully, stands up and stretches herself, shaking off her worries. "It's a deal!"

They drive along a country road, away from heavy thoughts, away from other people. There exist only Siv and Heinz and the humming car.

She leans happily back in the seat. She has no father or mother, no rejected Svend. There is only Heinz. Dear, sinful, understander-of-everything Heinz.

He drives to a remote inn.

Siv has no idea where they are. They left the main road a long time ago. They have driven along small, narrow roads, rushing past sheltered, sleepy farms.

She does not ask the name of the inn or where they are. It does not make the slightest difference to her!

"We'll spend the night here."

Heinz knows the place, drives the car into the courtyard and shows her the way into the dining room of the inn.

It is very comfortable and warm. The ceiling is whitewashed, low. The tables are of oak and without tablecloths.

Siv decides what they are to eat, Heinz, what they are to drink. The host comes over to their table and greets Heinz with a smile. He knows him. He has surely been here before—with other girls.

But that does not matter—not in the least!

Siv is hungry, happy and warm.

Heinz says strange, unbelievable things to her. Tells her that she is delightful, splendid—and she believes it all, believes that he really means it.

One thing is certain: There has never existed a girl like her, and there has never been a man so mortally in love.

Heinz leaves her for a moment, and she swims away into

her dreams about a future together with this man who knows the world, life, and her. When they go up to their room, she is encased in fog of sweet wine. This is reality. Everything which she has left behind her was only a bad dream.

It is only now that she has seriously begun to live—and see. The whole thing is beautiful, perfect.

The room is decorated with red roses. Heinz has put Indian incense in a small burner. The air is filled with a sweet, strange aroma. They turn off the electric light and put candles on the table instead. It is like a dream, a gentle magical dream, like a tale from *A Thousand and One Nights*.

He knows very well what can enchant a little, unexperienced, childish girl, this Heinz does. He makes her forget that life is more than love and incense, that ordinary days and a day of reckoning await them.

He suggests, "Let's take a bath."

She laughs. Whatever he wants to do, so does she.

They stand under the shower, close together in each others arms, and kiss while the water splashes over them. He holds her away from him and turns off the warm water so that only the cold streams down. She screams and gasps under the cold stream, kicks, claws, kicks. "Help!"

He turns off the water, dries her and crushes her against him. "You delightful little girl!"

She runs away from him and throws herself on the bed. "How warm you get after a cold shower."

He walks over to her and puts his hands around her laughing, trembling girlish body. "You don't need cold showers, because you are the hottest, most loving girl around."

And her world submerges, disappears in an intoxicating, bubbling, rushing roar of vibrating nerves and wild, animal bliss.

Siv is free—free—free!

Like the birds in God's heaven, like all of God's happy animals, which just screech, twitter and howl until they find a mate and consummate life's upsetting commandment.

She can behave just as she likes, say whatever she likes. She is endlessly happy. She is herself, completely herself, and completely honest.

Because nothing can shock this lover of hers who wants to escort her into the promised land. This lover who makes her scream, rejoice and groan.

During a short pause, she lies with her mouth and face hidden in the pit of his arm. She turns her face up toward him and laughs.

"What's so funny, child?"

"Oh, nothing. It's just that I'm completely and foolishly happy!"

CHAPTER TWENTY

Siv has to go to the yellow house.

Svend is sitting in the parlor. Her mother's eyes are swollen from crying. Siv feels no compassion.

Her father sits at his desk with his back to the room. That desk has always been his fortress.

A bookshelf hangs above the desk with pictures of the family: one of her father and mother as newlyweds, one of her father and mother with the baby Siv between them, all three smiling joyfully, and those of Siv alone, in all possible ages and situations—from the time she lay in a tiny diaper on the obligatory rug until the time she stood, a grown woman, in her hospital's uniform. The collection is finished, completed!

"Father! It's Siv!" Her mother calls weakly.

"Oh!"

A painful silence.

Then Siv says, and it sounds cuttingly hard in the quiet, "I can see that Svend has told you both everything. There was no need for me to come, then."

No answer.

"Well, I might just as well go."

Her father whips around in his chair. "You don't have to go."

His voice is soft, much too soft, and bitingly, snarlingly evil. Whenever he uses this tone he seems dreadful, hurting and sardonic.

His mouth moves away from his teeth in a strange grimace.

At this moment he does not look very much like a Christian.

But Siv's heart sorrows for him, searches for a sign,

proof that he understands her, that *something* in him understands her.

She wants to take his hands, kiss them, crush them in hers and worship them. She wants to let her fingers run along his taut, thick veins and bless his blood.

But she will never be able to do that.

A Christian God does not approve a gypsy's song, therefore he had to renounce it. Because Hell is awful. Hell is fire and brimstone and the tortures of the devil. Heaven is bliss and that is where your father is going when he is through with this crucible of life.

Little, brave, beloved father! You are not suited for the Christian heaven. You do not know it, but it won't be heaven as far as you are concerned.

"Father!" It is her mother's voice again. "Father, we'll have to talk nicely to her or else she'll just walk out again."

Siv stands with her back to the door. She has taken off her coat and stands with her hands in her pockets, looking at the various faces: There is Svend. His face is red and embarrassed. He has taken off his glasses and his heavy eyelids look naked and absurd.

"Svend, couldn't you have let me take care of this by myself?"

Her mother's voice breaks in, "Is there anything so strange about his feeling it necessary to talk to somebody? And who is closer to him than we are?"

Her father nods and his dark eyes are bright and hard. "I don't think that you have any right to reproach anybody, my dear."

Siv looks at him with wide-open, dry eyes and does not answer.

"He even says he's willing to go on with you, if *you* want to."

Siv bows her head. "*I* don't want to continue."

Her father stands up, plants himself in the middle of the floor. "Then we'll have to separate as well, I guess?"

Siv does not answer, just shrugs her shoulders.

Suddenly her mother sinks backwards in her chair with a weak groan.

Her father rushes over to her. So does Svend.

They lift her mother up and lay her on the divan.

Siv is still standing on the same spot. She has taken

her hands out of her pockets, stands there, swinging her arms as if she wants to help, but cannot.

Svend turns toward her. "Well, help your mother at least!"

She walks over and loosens her girdle, unbuttons the top of her dress so that Ino can breathe more freely and takes her pulse.

She is a patient!

Her father stands close behind her. She feels his excited breath on her neck. She stands completely still, with a freezing sensation down her back. Perhaps he is going to strike her in a moment or two?

Svend has fetched her mother's heart pills, and Siv gives them to her.

The worst is over now. Ino breathes more freely, and that awful rattling of her jaw has stopped.

She has a bad heart. She has had such attacks before, but never so powerfully.

Siv backs away and her father walks over to her mother, bends over her and carefully strokes her chubby hands. "There, there, Ino, everything will be all right."

Siv stands tense and silent. Do they expect her to fall down on her knees and beg forgiveness? Her mother expects it, and her father hopes that she will.

"Siv!" It is her mother's fearful voice. There is not just fear, there is also expectation: After all, she has done what she could to make Siv feel her guilt.

Nothing happens.

Siv looks at her father, stares him stiffly in the eyes and is unable to hide the terrible coldness she feels in her soul at this moment.

Then her father hoarsely snarls, "You hussy. You goddamn hussy! If your mother had died now, it would have been you who killed her."

Siv begins to cry inside herself.

Something has been betrayed, something between her and her father.

She turns her back on the room and walks out of the door.

The last thing she hears is a protesting whine from her mother.

Her father and Svend say nothing.

CHAPTER TWENTY-ONE

Siv takes her nursing examination two weeks later.

She has not gone back to the yellow house since the confrontation, nor has she seen Svend. She gets a letter from her mother. A sad, begging letter: They have forgiven their little girl. She *must* come back home to visit them. They will receive her with open arms. They pray for her—that Satan will not fool her—they pray *very often* for her. She knows how much they love her. But Siv cannot go home, not yet, and she cannot relieve her mother's sorrow. She has to go home some day, but that day will have to wait for a while. She is not yet able to smile at her father and mother.

Heinz visits her. He comes to her five out of the seven evenings in the week. He neglects his home, his children and his wife.

Siv is made uneasy by this thought. "Heinz, what does your wife say when you are never at home?"

"She doesn't say a thing, because she's never at home, either."

"Who looks after the children?"

"An old lady—and they really love *her*."

His voice turns very hard whenever he talks about his home. He explains that his wife, Greta Gertsen, is a dancer. She lives a lot in other towns and sleeps with other men.

Siv cannot understand. "Why do you stay married then?"

"Well, Siv, there are the children, you know—and she's a good companion."

A good companion? Yes, she would have to be—and yet?

Heinz cannot give her any better explanation, or perhaps he does not want to. He looks harassed and tired whenever Siv tries to learn more.

She gives up trying to penetrate this mystery. She is not

going to get married, neither to Heinz nor to anybody else. At least not now.

Every time he comes visiting he brings Siv something: wine, chocolate or flowers. He also brings paintings and rugs.

She has moved into a new room, the room for an assistant nurse. It is big and is in another building, and there is just one other person with whom she shares the kitchen.

She lives in this room among flowers, chocolates and expensive Persian rugs, among bronze statues and paintings.

Her ward, her room and Heinz! There is not much more in her life for the time being.

She does not want anything else during the first weeks. There is peace in this room which Heinz has stamped with his personality. There is peace in his calm, gentle, appreciating hands.

She stays away from her other acquaintances, away from her home. Lives under her lover with her ear against his beating heart.

The day she draws her first pay as assistant nurse, she feels herself to be marvelously rich: six hundred crowns and eighty-six öre! [$84.00] What is she to do with so much money? She rings Heinz and invites him to dinner.

Afterwards, she goes out to shop. What does he like? Oh, he's so spoiled! She buys food, wine (begging the wine merchant to give her the most suitable, the very best). She is nervous, happy and occupied. She indulges her whims and makes a noticeable dent in her rich purse.

Afterwards, she goes into the finest shop in town, buys a new dress and a golden, quilted kimono. She twists and turns in front of the large mirror. She now belongs to the demimonde; she is an experienced, calculating mistress. Oh, how beautiful she looks standing there wrapped in the seductive garb of a sinner. She can really understand why Heinz is so crazy about her.

They sit at the table. Siv has on her new dress.

She looks nervously at Heinz, watches every mouthful he takes, every gulp of wine he drinks. Do you think he likes it?

He looks smilingly at her. "You're great!"

"Yes, but the food. Does it taste all right?"

He laughs teasingly. "Didn't you hear what I said? You are goddamn great."

"Heinz, please—the food—is it all right?"

He laughs and nods, bends across the table and takes her hands: "Martha, Martha! You worry and get upset about many things, but I can tell you that one person at least is satisfied."

The food has been eaten, the wine has been drunk, all the words have been spoken!

Siv gets up and turns around in front of Heinz. "Do you like my dress? It's new."

"Yes, but I like you best without it."

"Very well, then, I'll take it off. You don't like my slip either, do you? And can't stand my panties."

She strips everything off at a breakneck speed, kicks the last bit away with her big toe, laughs and stretches her body, dizzy from the wine and her expectations.

"Come and take me, you big bull!"

Heinz has sat quietly looking at this stimulating performance. He now puts out his cigarette, slowly stands up and captures this naked, dancing girl. There is a strange, harassed expression on his face. "Yes, this is what you are, this is you, only you, you little gypsy!"

And he takes this naked truth into his possession.

Siv has completely forgotten about her seductive kimono.

CHAPTER TWENTY-TWO

A few weeks pass.

Siv beings to feel a restless burning in her body and soul: Is this all? Shouldn't she be beginning to live *now?*

She has only a dim idea of what it is that she wants.

But it is something festive and happy, with lots of people, a swarming mass of people. They are to meet in small groups at various tables, they are to look at each other, scrutinize each other and talk so that the words just fly. They are to laugh together, dance together and cry together.

They are to be intoxicated and say funny things, they are to be sober and indignant.

There must be *all* kinds of people present if Siv is to "live the life."

Shouldn't Heinz show her this life?

But Heinz has become a lonely man—and he drags Siv with him into his loneliness.

Doesn't he have any friends? Any interesting acquaintances?

He takes her out to the movies, the theater and concerts. He knows the actors—and actresses! Siv has an idea that he knows some of them *very* well.

He knows a lot about music, knows names, compositions, opus numbers. He explains the whole thing until she gets all confused.

She likes music, but she has always just listened to it without thinking about who composed one thing or another.

She cannot bring herself to try to learn. She nods as if she understands and is interested whenever Heinz engagingly explains. But she just listens to the music, hears only the notes, and fastens her eyes on the most handsome man among the musicians. The technical information just slips right out of her head.

He takes her with him to painting exhibitions and explains the paintings to her. She listens, trying to seem interested, but most of the paintings leave her cold. They are, at any rate, no match for nature.

Once there is a picture which attracts her, excites her. It is from Italy: You see a young mother with her child. They sit beneath a sun-bathed, golden wall. She remains standing in front of this picture, completely captivated. How healthy and happy they look! And what colors! No colors excite Siv so much as yellow and gold do.

Heinz looks at her with interest. "Yes, it's beautiful, isn't it?"

He drags her away to other things. Since she understands this one painting, she must also be able to understand something else.

She stares blindly at old paintings in dark, dull colors, at portraits where the eyelids are thick and heavy. At cloth in dresses which shines like velvet embroidered with golden thread. She thinks they look stiff and dead.

But she says nothing of this to Heinz. She is the one who is stupid, isn't she?

One day she sees an exhibition by a famous Danish surrealist.

Heinz looks questioningly and smilingly at her face as she observes the paintings. He knows the painter, greets him. He is a dark, delicate man with fantastically bright, shining eyes.

Siv wanders around looking at the exhibition by herself.

Her first thought is: "No, how ugly all this is!"

There are portraits of women with their stomachs cut up, with breasts with strange things growing on them, with hands that end in claws and branches. An eye sits on a stalk and develops into many unusual things. There are fantastic landscapes with woods of gigantic, penis-like columns. There are deathbeds with grinning devils and pious nuns, with bats and other strange things.

And there is a picture called "Sabotage." You see a disgusting little man on the top of a frightening cliff. He looks down into a dark, deep chasm.

Both Heinz and the artist come over to her: Well?

Both ask, and they both look at her as if they knew much more about her than she knew herself.

She will not answer, because she does not know what she thinks of all of this.

The painter says, "You are too young. You are too young. You don't understand this, but one day you will."

She nods. "Perhaps."

Yes, Siv experiences quite a lot—but always alone with Heinz.

One evening he takes her out to an expensive restaurant.

A well-known gypsy orchestra is to play that evening. Heinz knows this, and he also knows that Siv loves such music.

"Eat, child, eat and drink!"

She drinks a little, eats a little—listens.

She forgets Heinz, forgets the strained, wise world she has landed in. She remembers only that she has heard these sounds before.

Her father, Sacho, could have played with this orchestra. He *should* have been there. As first violinist!

And she? She belongs to these dark, sweaty, excited men in red jackets. She listens to the sobbing, sentimental, caressing, arousing rhythms!

They sit at a table near the orchestra. She looks at the man who plays first violin, meets his eyes and holds them fast—or is it he who holds her eyes captive?

He turns completely toward her and plays, smiles a little, and plays—she thinks—*just* for her.

His pants are so tight that you can see the outline of his genitals, and the strong legs move rhythmically to the music.

They play *"Hotiyania!"*

She wants to go up to him, she wants to get away—away from the white hands that want to show her the pale fruits of the tree of knowledge. She wants to go up to this man—and *live*.

Heinz nudges her. "Where are you?"

She returns. "I'm here, of course!"

"No, you're not!"

He looks at her dark, shining eyes, at her trembling mouth and her vibrating nostrils. "No, you were committing adultery with that violinist!"

He laughs a little. He is not annoyed, is not jealous. He looks at her admiringly and with pleasure.

And Siv is embarrassed and angry because she feels as if her soul is naked. It does not matter if your body is naked, not if it is beautiful. But your soul must be covered! Because it is not very lovely, not Siv's. Heinz is not allowed to see her like this! Why not? She has told him so much about herself, hasn't she?

She doesn't know why not! But the man up there with the violin, he can look at her. He would just have laughed, and would have taken her, strong and healthy. He would not have given a thought to her soul, he did not want to be *in love* with her.

Siv is silent on the way home.

"You are so quiet. What are you thinking about?"

"Heinz, couldn't we be together with other people, every now and then? Don't you know anybody you can introduce me to?"

They walk on for a while in silence. She looks up at Heinz. He looks withdrawn and bitter.

"Siv, there is no pleasure in getting to know other people. Sooner or later you'll be dreadfully disappointed. I *know!*"

"You have known many, then?"

"Yes, I have."

After a while he says, "Yes, the better you get to know people, the more you come to prefer animals. A worn-out cliché, child, but true!"

She does not answer. She is silent and sad.

Perhaps he is right. He is always right. But she wants to find out for herself. She does not want to be locked out of life because of his experiences. She does not want to share his bitterness, because she does not feel any bitterness. She wants to love, live and learn. He has no right to pull her into his loneliness, to use her like a refreshing aperitif for the grayness of everyday and an unsuccessful marriage.

What is it that he always says when he comes to visit her? "Oh, I am always in a good mood when I'm together with you."

He wants to use her, bit by bit. Make her wise on the basis of his own experiences and guard her as her father, her mother and Svend have guarded her.

But she will not believe him. She will not believe anyone any more, if she does not feel the truth inside of herself.

She will not hate the Jews because he does, will not believe that Negroes are animals. She will not learn to turn her nose up at what Heinz calls "the Proletariat." She wants to mix with them, have them crowd around her, find out who smells good, and she will smile to some and open her hands—and her thighs.

Doesn't Heinz give her enough love?

How much is enough?

He undresses her, takes her in his arms and lays her down on the bed. He puts his hands around her small, firm breasts and says, "Look, exactly one handful for each hand."

Oh, his hands! They are beautiful, long, white and flexible. He is proud of his hands. She has seen him roll a coin between his fingers, elegantly and quickly, so that she was almost unable to follow it with her eyes.

These hands of his stroke down along her flanks, her stomach, they find every nerve in her sensitive body. Her skin quivers like that of a mare bitten by a fly. She laughs in ecstasy, enjoying it, because she has quivering nerves everywhere.

And when he lies on top of her, firmly and triumphantly in her narrow sex, he laughs gently and happily, takes her head between his hands and kisses her softly and adoringly.

He never forgets himself. He only thinks of her—only of her. He watches to see that she is enjoying it and sees how she reacts, listens to her screams, before his own reach his throat.

Isn't he the perfect lover, then?

Yes, he is, and anybody who says anything else will be a liar. He gives more than he takes. Thinks more of his woman than he thinks of himself.

What else can a girl ask for? What else? Yes, what else?

She gathers into her hands all that she knows about Heinz. It is an unusual bouquet.

It is beautiful and disgusting: He hates Jews, hates Negroes. He is pleased whenever he can read about their subjugation.

But she has been in his car and watched him drive carefully around a wood snail. And he loves her.

Siv does not understand him. She cannot understand him, even if she wanted to with her whole heart.

He reads a lot: literature which is ugly and grotesque— but also beautiful, warm descriptions about *The Life of a Country Squire*.

He drinks in distorted, mocking surrealism—but stands enrapt in front of velvet-painted old masters.

She does not understand him.

Siv thinks of all of this the evening she walks home with Heinz after the exciting gypsy concert. This is why she is silent—and sad.

She says good night to him—without taking off her clothes. She says that she is tired.

He looks nervously at her and goes, hoping that she will soon be feeling better.

She takes out a piece of stationery and her pen. She will write to Copenhagen to ask for a job in one of the hospitals there.

She has to get away from this town, away from the yellow house that gnaws in her mind like a persistent worm. She has to get away from Heinz and his wise, suggestive words, from all her memories and her great confusion.

She must leave—just leave.

CHAPTER TWENTY-THREE

Siv goes home to her father and mother to tell them about her decision.

Her father does not say very much. He looks old.

He looks gently and carefully at her, so sadly that Siv forgets the harsh words said on the day of reckoning.

He sits at the kitchen table and lays his hands carefully together. He has promised God and himself that he will control himself.

"So, you want to go to Copenhagen?"

"Yes."

"What about this Heinz of yours?"

"He's married, you know."

Her father bites his lip. It is difficult for him to control himself.

"This Heinz, yes, this Heinz."

"Father, it wasn't he who turned me into a different person. It's not his fault. It would have happened anyway."

Sacho mumbles, "I'm not so sure of that."

Siv leans passionately forward. "You have no right to judge him—because—because—he loves me."

"Does he want to marry you?"

It comes dry and hard.

"Yes, but I don't want to marry him."

"*You* don't want to?" Her father nods, grunts, controls himself. "So that's what you are then—*my* daughter."

She answers, trembling, "Yes, your daughter."

Sacho has lowered his head. He cracks his knuckles in bitter doubt. "God will help us."

Siv's voice becomes soft. "Yes, He will, Father."

God will help them, because it is He who is to judge, not Father Sacho.

She now sees that her father is little—and very old.

Heinz sits in Siv's room and looks heavily at her. "So, you want to go to Copenhagen to get to know other men?"

"No—o."

"Oh, yes, you do," he says, and there is a mocking resignation in his voice.

"That's not the most important reason, Heinz."

But he will not understand this. He can, but he won't. She explains, apologizes, swears.

He does not want to understand.

"You can come and visit me. It doesn't mean much for you to fly to Copenhagen."

"Yes, I've already thought of coming."

She tries to smile happily. "Well, then, you see that things aren't as bad as they seem."

"No."

No, is this anything to complain about? This is no worse than it usually is when you have found your life and lost it again.

Do you have to make so much out of it?

He helps her with her preparations, gives her good advice.

But he looks sick and cannot control his face.

Goodbye, Heinz—and thanks a lot.

You taught me a lot. You opened the way to the kingdom of love. You escorted me into this kingdom with gentle, loving hands. And you taught me to think. At any rate, you wanted to teach me to think. But I am so young that all I can do is *feel*.

Siv sits on the train on her way to Copenhagen.

She is not unhappy, just melancholy.

She is a little surprised at herself: She ought to feel more regret, be more afraid, oughtn't she? She is going out into an unknown world now, completely alone. But a wall has grown up about her soul.

It grew up with her, became greater when she met Svend.

Sacho's God and the twisting, holy women, Siv's desire for piety, ground the wall round and smooth, but did not knock it down.

In spite of embroidery and hypocrisy, painted lips and hymns, the wall grew, solidly and calmly.

Then there were her begging prayers for forgiveness and cradle-like dreams at night, something the Christians called "self-contamination."

Heinz locked the wall around her!

Now she is alone—with herself.

And *it is a wonderful, peaceful thing.*

PART TWO

CHAPTER ONE

Siv sits, depressed, on her wide divan and *wants* to be happy. She is now living in Cophenhagen. She has found herself a job in a surgical ward, a large ward with fifty nurses and twenty doctors. She has been received in a friendly way and has gotten into the swing of things. She has also found herself an efficiency apartment near the hospital. Her apartment is on the fourth floor of a new building and consists of a kitchen, an entrance hall and a large room with bright windows and walls. There are yellow tiles in the bathroom and the kitchen has a garbage chute and a refrigerator. Yes, Siv lives comfortably. She has bought her furniture on the installment plan, because you cannot live in an empty apartment. She has bought curtains and flowers and decorated the apartment with the rugs and paintings Heinz gave her. She has also bought a combination radio-phonograph, shrugging her shoulders at the thought of all the time payments. It will all work out. She makes a lot of money now, over seven hundred crowns [$100] a month, and that's a terrible lot of money.

She had no time at all to think during the first days. She shopped, straightened things out, arranged things, was happy and occupied.

But now everything is in shipshape order, and she sits down and looks around with pleasure and can say what the Lord said after he had created the earth and Adam and Eve: "It is good."

After she had bought the wide sofa and placed it in the living room, she sat on it, bounced on it, stroked it with pleasure. "Now we two are going to experience Copenhagen."

But now she sits on it and begins to think: "Is everything so wonderful after all? Yes, it is." She does not wish to listen to any depressing murmur about loneliness. She will not admit it. Now she has things just the way she has always wanted them, just what she has fought for and dreamed of.

She has the freedom to do what she wants, think what she wants and say what she thinks. But to whom is she going to say it? She does not know anybody. What is she going to do now? It is eight o'clock in the evening. She can read, listen to the radio, smoke or go for a walk, can't she? But she needs another person, many people, feels the need for laughter and loud talking, parties and fun, new amusing experiences.

She also needs a man, a lover, a strong fellow with hair on his chest and a song in his body. She also needs quiet, intimate conversations, caresses, tenderness and strength.

She has only herself, and, for the time being, she is deathly tired of herself, of seeing her own lips in the mirror when she makes herself up, looking into her own, stupid eyes which thought that they knew so much and could do so many things. She is tired of her transparent, short, seductive nightgown. Tired of brushing her shiny hair which no one will muss up or run his fingers through. She is thoroughly tired of her well-kempt self which only waits to be used, raped, crushed and misused in the strangest ways.

She grabs her thighs with her small, brown hands, her smooth, round thighs which are neither too thick nor too thin. They are just as they should be.

Damn. Siv stretches. She waits, waits with her body, soul and senses for—Copenhagen.

Isn't it here that you can find lots of small places with spiritual artists, soulful talk and wise free-thinking ideas? Isn't this the city where you learn to know both the good and evil sides of life?

Copenhagen, the Paris of the North, the city of the king and the Royal Guards, the city of passions and pimps, the city of bars and wild night life. The city of tolerance and wit. Where bells ring, where people swarm, where neon signs flash and gleam.

And here sits a long-legged girl with her yearning for experience and life—and cannot find a way into the city.

She is lonely.

She lies down, angry and unhappy and without looking into the mirror. She takes out a book, but cannot bring herself to read it, lies in the dark and smokes.

Heinz had told her so very much about this city. He had spent his youth here, his stretch in the army and that period filled with strength when a man can do anything if he just expands his chest and breathes deeply.

Life is delightful. Period. It is, because that is what Siv has decided it is to be. Something will surely happen tomorrow. Because Copenhagen is delightful, and Siv will discover it, of course she will.

She digs herself into her pillow, closes her eyes, puts her hands between her legs and goes to sleep in obstinate expectation.

She appears on her job the next morning fresh and assured, puts on her uniform and her friendly role. She has to do so if she is going to get along with her acquaintances and colleagues.

She ties her apron tightly about her hips so that everybody can see how slim she is. She sets her hair up under her cap and looks fresh, clean and attractive. She says good morning to everyone, looks eager to work, as she trips out into the hall with strength tingling in her body and fingers. Now there is work to be done, a new exciting day has begun. So much can happen in a new, long day. She stands together with her sister nurses and studies the black notice board where all the day's operations are posted. She looks into the book to see which room she is to be in today and finds out which doctor she is to assist. She enjoys herself.

Is work a curse? Who has said so? No, it is wonderful; it gives the movements of your body some meaning, some reason for the use of your strength. If work is God's curse on mankind, how great a thing a blessing must be.

Siv walks into her room. She is alone and quickly glances around the room, looks at her orders and sets out the instruments. She fetches trays and implements, orders and arranges them in the way she thinks most practical. She walks out into the hall and gives the first patient a hand. She smiles at him with a smile that causes the poor, pained, nervous fellow to jump. It shines in his face with warm pleasure. She is quite aware of the way she is smiling, but she cannot control herself. Her smile bursts out of her mouth and eyes and her entire pliant body.

When she smiles like this it is not because she wants to, but simply because she cannot help herself. She has had too much put into her, she has to get rid of some of her capital.

The patient blinks his eyes and smiles back: What a sweet nurse. Perhaps it won't hurt so much after all?

Well, it may very well happen that it does hurt. It is quite possible that it will hurt a lot. Siv feels compassion like a warm stream in her throat. It makes her voice a little huskier and her eyes a little brighter. Because she frequently feels so sorry, so heartrendingly sorry for other people. But she never feels sorry for herself.

She is healthy—thank God.

She is young—thank God.

Some day—many years from now—she too will surely be sick, but that day is so far, far away that she cannot finish the thought.

She is a queen in her room. It is her responsibility that things go as they should, that the doctors are satisfied with her help and are given precisely the instruments they are to use. This is her responsibility and her pride. She walks calmly and carefully about—the perfect nurse.

The patients hold her hand tightly, look at her with touching confidence: What a clean, smart, calm nurse, who knows all about these shiny instruments and strange things, and who feels herself so much at home and is so experienced in the operating room with its green tiles and its white table.

She nods reassuringly to them, sets things in order, is completely aware of her own importance and enjoys the warming glances from admiring patients and students. Yes, of course she is a wonderful nurse.

She walks around smiling somewhat ironically to herself. But the smile remains behind her white uniform and her professional air.

Don't you realize that I am just a human being like you? A tiny, little human being, an ant in the great ant hill, the earth? Oh, you all think that I am very clever because you can't do this yourselves. But you know, I am almost unable to fill out my income-tax return. I can't add or subtract and can walk thoughtfully around in a store, looking around, although there is absolutely nothing in the store for me to buy. And I am cheated when I shop because I cannot add.

Do you realize that I am a woman underneath my uniform? Do you understand? Do you understand—a real woman? With vices and virtues—mostly the former. I would like to creep under the protection of a man's strength; I would let him do what he liked if he was really a man. I would say yes and amen to everything he said. I would look admiringly at him and worship his understanding of politics and business—if he would just take care of me and my practical things. My papers authorizing my transfer of residence are not in order. I completely forgot about them, and now I'm going to have to pay a large fine. One day I'm sure to get a letter asking me to report to some bewildering place or other to look into stern faces which are completely unimpressed by my kingdom here in the operating room.

Architect—that is what is written in the patient's day book. He lies there with pained, brown eyebrows. He is good at mathematics. If he only knew how stupid she had been at school!

But it is me, Siv, who rules now. You are nervous and upset because you are sick. The devil laughs and crushes your pride. You have no use for your mathematical calculations. You are sick and therefore only a human being.

Do not look at me like that. Do not believe that I am an angel, a smart, awe-inspiring angel who stands, in the most difficult moment, prepared with the wisest weapon. I am only a woman, and if you were healthy, you could take me, subjugate me and rule over me. Because you are a man. I can see that, even though you are sick.

Siv puts a pillow beneath the injured leg, sticks a hypodermic in that strong arm, smiles reassuringly and fixes the salt-water tank and the table of instruments.

The patient follows her movements like a dog following those of his master, and Siv is important and very lonely beneath her professional veneer.

She gossips with her sister nurses during the morning break, but only laughter, jokes and shop talk are exchanged between her and them. The others are already friends, groups of two, three or four. They go into town together in the evening, have met one another's boy friends and friends, and whisper together the following day at the breakfast table.

Siv smiles agreeably and retreats. It is of no concern of hers what they talk about.

They talk about George, Jørgen and Einar, while they put on their regular clothes. They look at Siv's tight slacks and blouse. "How well-dressed you are, Siv."

Siv answers, "Yes." Brushes her hair down to her shoulders, puts on some more lipstick and looks at herself in the mirror, seeing a young, busy girl who is going into Copenhagen with all of its experiences. She walks over to the door and waves a smiling goodbye.

Oh, yes, they think, she is clever, and they can also get to like her, can't they? Of course, she feels that they can, as friends at work.

But there is a difference between her and them, all the same.

Her colleagues look like nurses—even in their regular clothes. They resemble small ladies. They pull their silk stockings up over their legs, their corsets over their stomachs and trip away on high-heeled shoes in street clothes and a hat—perhaps gloves as well. They show each other the latest models of blouses, coats and undergarments.

Siv never wears a hat, never has gloves on her brown hands with their bright red nail polish. She tosses her hair around her neck and steps out in long slacks, wearing loafers, and, if it is summer, as it is now, she just has on sandals without stockings.

She *has* a nice street dress and high-heeled shoes as well; she has tried to dress up when she goes to work. She has enjoyed the approving cries of her comrades: "How pretty you look when you dress up."

But what a lot of trouble it is. Think, to put on all of that just for a ten-minute walk to the hospital.

The next day she stubbornly puts on her slacks again.

And if she has to make a trip into town? My, how tired you get, all covered up like a lady.

And then, there is another thing, something quite different and very important: The right men do not look at her when she is dressed up like a lady—and those that do, do not look at her in the right way.

But these are things that you do not tell your friends; you do not tell them to anybody. Because it is too foolish.

No, you turn around a little, wrinkle your forehead and say stubbornly, "I dress the way I want to. I feel better in long slacks and flat shoes."

She knows that her acquaintances talk about her. They believe that she has so many invitations to go out that she almost cannot accept them all. But they also think that she is a little too improper, a little too provocative in her clothes and her manner of acting. They think all this—with a trace of envy or doubt.

But Siv wants to be the person she *is*. She is filled with a stubborn defiance whenever someone tries to change her. She is secretly thrilled with herself and takes it as a compliment whenever a man can look at her and see that here is a girl who is willing.

CHAPTER TWO

Siv is again sitting at home in the evening. She has put a record of Tchaikovsky on the record player, has opened up a new pack of cigarettes. She has gone to the library the previous day and taken out a whole pile of books. They are mostly books about travel. One day she is going to travel and see the whole world. Go to Egypt and see the pyramids, look up into the face of the unfathomable Sphinx, go to Africa and rumple the dark curly hair of a little Negro boy, go to China and curtsey low for an honorable mandarin.

For a while she forgets about her uneasy loneliness, smokes and reads.

What time is it now? Only nine?

She stretches herself and notices a tingling uneasiness in her body. It is very strange; is this how one lives in a big city where there are lots of people?

She looks at her divan and smiles ironically to herself: She had thought that she would be able to find a man very quickly in Copenhagen, a man for her, one who would think it wonderful to visit her place and her divan, one who would lift her up into the seventh heaven and leave her with a smile and a thank you. That must be a delightful arrangement for a man, don't you think? A girl who does not want to get married and does not ask for promises, but just wants to swing in time with him as long as it lasts.

Heinz, you are far away up there on your high peak of experience. What would you make of all this? Am I still delightful? Why can't I find anybody—a man? Do I long for you? Yes, I do. I long to tell you about this and hear your explanation. I long for a person to love me. It is cowardice, I know. Now, I am all by myself, just as I wanted to be, and I have to discover everything on my own.

She puts on her jacket and decides to go for a walk.

Not a single evening goes by in which Siv does not go for a walk. It becomes a desperate vice for her to take a walk late at night. She walks up and down the streets, around corners, over roads and squares.

She encounters many men on these evening walks of hers. They look at her with interest as she passes them. She looks quickly at them—and walks on. What else can she do? But couldn't it happen that there are other people walking the streets for the same reason? Someone who is just as lonely and starving?

And couldn't it be possible that one of these is meant for her?

But if a man speaks to her, he is usually drunk or looks stupid and speaks with a slow, ugly accent.

Young men shout, whistle and act silly and they do not interest her. They invite her to dances, the movies or restaurants. They will tell their stupid jokes and shyly kiss her goodbye at her street door, while they agree upon another date. Then there are the soldiers. They are just not to be tolerated, because they are not normal human beings when they walk along gathered into a flock, wearing the same uniform on their bodies.

There are small, fat men, with narrow, satiated eyes. Tall, thin men with sway backs and wretched coats. They look sickly at her and give up before they have thought the thought.

Then there are the gay businessmen who come out of warm, well-lit places, with their coats unbuttoned and their hats on a slant, smoking cigars.

They look at her with pleasure as they pass her, say something to a colleague and walk on, filled with cognac and solid business deals: a sweet tart, something you enjoy looking at, but you haven't time for more.

There are also men who get nervous when they look at her. Their eyes fly out of control: This girl is too demanding.

Siv pulls her jacket around her. No, it must be stupid to have the idea that you can find a man in the streets. She walks quickly home, puts her key in the door and lets her body into the warm room. How can she be so foolish? To throw away an entire evening wandering around looking for something which cannot be found *there*.

It is one o'clock at night. She has to hurry to bed. She has to be at work at seven in the morning. She crawls under her blanket and feels very stupid.

She tosses and turns, cannot sleep, lights a cigarette, and bitter, angry thoughts begin to tumble around in her head.

Civilization has stuck cotton in men's ears, made their eyes polite and frightened, paralyzed their tongues and their hands.

They stand along the streets with taut, strained bulges in their pants. They look at the girls, from the front, from behind. They imagine themselves already inside them, imagine that they move their feet to pursue, raise their hands to stop the object of their desire.

But they just sigh and remain standing where they are.

The woman sees their eyes as she walks past them. For a short moment both of them shiver a little, then she walks on, feeling the man's eyes on her back. Her body sways a little, straightens up, gets a conscious rocking movement.

Does anything happen? Does anything happen? Does anything happen?

No. No. Nothing happens.

Because they are all well-bred people, they are civilized.

It is the man's duty just to look with admiration, it is the girl's duty to walk on, quickly and nervously. What if he should speak to her? What if his desire overcame his politeness? Then she is supposed to close her eyes, shake her head and rush away. She has to go home and say that some disgusting and shabby man had embarrassed her with a dirty proposition.

Oh, how lovely it is to hide yourself in a cloak of annoyance when you do not have to listen and do what nature incites you to do.

Just go on and cry, you little, confused girl and all of you big, polite men.

Couldn't you have approached that woman? Perhaps she had an engagement.

Maybe, but then, couldn't she just smile and say "No, thanks?"

No, things don't work out that way; you know very well that that is not how she would react. She would think

"What an idiotic man this man must be; perhaps he is also drunk." Something could be wrong with him—and he could also make her pregnant, couldn't he?

Or else: If she says yes—or even maybe—what wouldn't he think of her later? He would not consider her to be of much worth, nothing more than a slut.

And you don't want to be considered a slut. You want to be considered a civilized human being.

Yes, that is how things are. The Christian Bible says that there is a place called hell, an awful, heartrending hell. A place where there is an endless Mardi Gras with masks, closed eyes and smiles. Behind the masks lie soft, vulnerable flesh, warm blood, fearful lusts, unutterable dreams and a bad conscience.

Behind the masks, yes, behind the masks.

But no one ever looks behind the masks, because they can never be taken off. They are glued on with the thick, sticky glue of fear. They make the thin skin underneath bleed. But they cannot, must not be removed.

Because what would we see then? A naked face, which is shocking because it is *human*.

This hell makes life incomprehensible.

Siv fusses with her cigarette in the ashtray, slowly and emphatically. Something must be done about this civilization, with its mistakes and incomprehensible things which create untieable knots in men's minds. But how?

Siv suddenly sits up in bed, lights a new cigarette with shaking fingers: Now she knows—you could *write* about it. You could write about people, as they are—and not as they want to be. Yes, you could do that. But how do you get started? With yourself? She winces a bit. Yes, you will have to start with yourself and your own desires. That is probably the safest and the most honest way of going about it.

She begins to speculate as to how much a typewriter costs; it can also be bought on the installment plan, can't it? She puts out the next cigarette, turns resolutely over on her side, because the decision has been made: Tomorrow she is going to go down to buy a typewriter, teach herself to type—you can surely buy instruction manuals. Then she will have something to occupy herself with during the long nights. She will no longer walk the streets searching for something. She will not search at all. One day it will surely come to her, all the wonderful things she longs for. And in the meantime, she will write. It must be easy to write, if you write in the same way that you think. But could she get it published?

Ha! She jumps up in bed. If she has a book published some day, she will send it to Heinz. Perhaps she will also write to him and tell him that she has started to write. He'll be proud that he has known her. He'll say to himself, "I knew it. I understood it the first time I saw Siv—she's not an ordinary woman; she's an artist."

Siv snuggles down into her pillow, bends her legs in excited expectation, already feels herself standing on a peak of fame and admiration.

But she is going to write because she wants to help mankind get around the sharp, cutting corners of civilization, isn't she? Yes, of course, she hasn't forgotten—but it would also be nice if she could become famous at the same time.

She can understand much better why she has had such an awful time, is so lonely and misunderstood. Artists have always had an awful time; if they don't, then they are not really artists.

Siv falls asleep with a happy smile on her lips.

CHAPTER THREE

The next day, when Siv is finished with her work, she goes out to buy a typewriter. She wants to test it in the store.

A very natural thing to do, isn't it?

She sits at a little table with a burning redness in her cheeks, then she quickly gets up. "I have to learn how to type first, so I would like to have an instruction manual, if you have any."

The man smiles—is he just smiling, or is he laughing? Siv tries to stand proudly. There is nothing shameful in her not being able to type. There are many people who can't. She just entered the store in the wrong way, wrapped in a golden fog of dreams, like a famous and discriminating author who could only type on the very best machine.

She tumbles out of the store with the brown case, holding it by the handle. She turns and smiles an embarrassed farewell. The man stands behind the windowpane looking smilingly at her with both hands in his pockets. Why did he stand there with his hands in his pockets? He looked so mocking and superior, didn't he?

He was probably just happy to have sold something. Siv forgets her painful blushes. She rushes home, locks her door, sets the case on the table and carefully takes the machine out, very carefully, as if it were a little child.

There it is, black, shiny and very promising.

Siv feels a shiver go down her spine. She runs her fingers over the keys, steps back a little and looks at it. She has also bought paper. She unpacks this and with great difficulty manages to insert a sheet of paper into the machine, pulls over a chair, sits down—and stops cold. She remembers that she cannot type.

She begins slowly, with one finger: "I am now going to write a book about what kind of a person I am and what I think other people are like."

It takes a long, long time to write just these few words.

She takes out her instruction manual and begins to practice with ten resisting fingers. After half an hour, she gets up, stretches, laughs at the machine, grates her teeth, raises her eyebrows and looks steadily and threateningly at it. "I'll learn how to type. Yes, you all can rest assured" (she says this to the collected peoples of the world) "that I'll learn how to type. You'll see, some day I'm going to write a book that will explode—with all that I want to say."

She leaves the room and fixes herself some food, has suddenly become ravenously hungry, singing as she cooks.

Life has again been given a purpose, because here she stands, the newly hatched author dreaming herself into authorship.

One evening Siv has typed for four hours. It is nine o'clock, and, feeling heaviness in her head, she decides she needs some fresh air. She puts on her coat and goes out for a walk.

Half an hour later she is sitting in a sidewalk café in the square facing the City Hall. She has ordered a beer, has drunk it and now sits rolling the empty glass between her hands, looking out at the delightful square with all its neon signs and its talkative mass of people. She deliberates as to whether she wants another glass or not. Should she pay, get up and go home and try to type some more? She can also go to bed. It is a pleasure to write, but it is a lonely pleasure. She looks down at her hand holding the glass: It is cold and empty, this glass, it is dead. She longs for something warm to hold.

She suddenly hears a rustling noise at the side of her table. She turns abruptly; there is a man standing in front of her. He has put a hand on her table, bows a little, smiles. Her eyes glance quickly over his entire body. He is probably thirty years old, strong, solid and well-built, his skin is tanned and weatherbeaten, clean as only the sun and the sea can make it. And he is smiling at Siv with a crooked, foxy smile, a bit embarrassed. He raises one of his eyebrows in an amusing arch. "My name is Lars Thompsen. May I offer you a drink?"

She nods with a smile: Of course, if he wants to.

He pulls over a chair and sits down in front of her, waves for the waiter, orders and, afterwards, folds his hands upon the tablecloth as if he wanted to say: That's *that.* He smiles and looks at her with pleasure and contentment.

And Siv laughs. She does not really know why she laughs, but she feels a warm, chuckling joy in her body which has to come out one way or another.

He stretches his hand across the table and grabs hers. "I'm a sailor, but I'm not sailing at the moment." He wrinkles his brow and quickly explains that certain family problems make it necessary for him to be at home for a while.

So the formalities are over. Siv has told him her name. They have shaken hands, and his hand remains on top of hers on the table.

A pair of hands are much better than words, much better. Her hand flutters like a baby bird inside this new warmth. She looks at him, looks down again, smiles a trembling smile which ripples the corners of her mouth: Thank God, she does not look like a lady this evening.

He has a tattoo on the back of his hand, a ship with an anchor.

An unknown man with a song in his body.

She does not know him, but he is warm and close and *her type.*

They drink up and walk over to the Tivoli amusement park. They knock down dishes and ride the roller coaster; Siv howls and lets him put his arms protectingly around her. At midnight they watch the fireworks.

He has such a funny, crooked eyebrow, this Lars. Siv has looked at it so often that she finally touches it with his finger and explains, "It was scarred once when I was in a fistfight. Therefore I always look as if I'm winking at all the girls."

She laughs. "And you probably do, too."

"Only if they are pretty." He looks at her, bites his lips together for joy over his catch. His suntanned face is warm and honest.

When they come out of the gates, he stops, puts a hand on her neck. "You'll come home with me, won't you?"

She hesitates, because that is what you are supposed to do. He fans his fingers out and lets them run through her hair, tries to capture her eyes, does not repeat his question.

She still does not answer, but, then, she does not have to.

They walk silently through the city side by side.

Lars has a nice place. Large, comfortable easy chairs, many unique things from strange countries—rugs, pillows, figurines—and everything smells of dust, tobacco, newspapers—and man. Lars rushes about. "What will you have, straight whiskey or a cocktail?" Siv tells him. She sinks down into a deep easy chair and enjoys the active man in the plaid shirt with the rolled-up sleeves. Do you think he is just as brown, has just as many strong muscles over the rest of his body?

He walks toward a door. "Where are you going?" "Just a minute—it will only take a minute. I'll be right back." He disappears into the kitchen—and returns a while later with a large tray. "Help yourself, dear lady. I hope that you're hungry." She sniffs at the tray: thick slices of French bread, liver paste, an opened can of shrimps, warm, bursting sausages.

Oh, yes, she is hungry, ravenously hungry and happy, gay as a lass of sixteen who is about to experience something exciting for the first time. She gobbles the food, talks, drinks, laughs at the man who sits across from her, warm and full of expectation. She has forgotten her loneliness, forgotten all her long walks to try to find the right man, because here he is, right in front of her. He drinks with her, and his gray eyes sparkle with warm curiosity. She throws her legs over the arm of the chair, lets her sandals fall to the floor, sinking down into a quiet happiness with a cigarette and a piece of chocolate.

"Tell me, are you always so well supplied? You must be used to walking the streets picking up poor, lonely, hungry girls and taking them home."

He becomes serious, looks questioningly at her. "Do you really have no boy friend?" She shakes her head, her mouth full of chocolate.

"You see—you understand—" It comes out hesitantly, somewhat embarrassed, "I don't want to get in anybody's way." Siv cringes a little. "No, I'm free for the time being." She has become serious, is about to begin remembering.

He discovers her seriousness, stands up, throws out his hands, looks at her with a big smile. "Shall we play a game? We are the only people left in the world, and we are stranded on a deserted island." He wrinkles his eyebrows. "And what in hell does a sailor do when he is stranded on a deserted island with a delightful girl?"

He has walked over to the other end of the room. "Come here to me!"

Siv looks at him with annoyance. Is it going to take such a long time, he postponed still more, this delightful thing which is about to happen? "I can't. I've drowned here in this chair."

"Oh, yes, you can. Come on. Come on!"

He snaps his fingers, calling on her like a little dog. "Come on. Come on!"

"Well, I guess I'll have to try."

She breathes heavily and groans, makes a lot of needless movements and finally manages to draw her body up out of the chair.

She then stands a few yards from him, in her stockings and mussed up hair. She raises her eyes up to him without raising her head. "Shall we meet halfway?"

"No, come on!" He stands there laughing with joy. "Closer. Closer." He puts his hands on his hips, taps his foot on the floor. "You can still come much closer."

Siv walks right up to him, puts her chin against his chest, grinds her nose into his body and bites him through his thin shirt.

"What the hell!" He throws his arms around her, crushing her to him, shakes her head back so that her thick, black hair flies away from her face. Looks down into her half-serious, half-smiling flushed face.

Then he picks her up and walks around with her as if she were a little child, carries her into another room, holds her high over the bed and lets her fall. He sits down beside her, puts his hands around her hips, strokes his lips over her neck, whispers with a voice smothered by her mussed hair, "How silly you were to come home with me, because now I'm going to eat you up."

She sits in the middle of the bed, with her arms around his knees and her chin resting on them. She is smoking and amuses herself by blowing streams of smoke over his stomach. The smoke breaks up into strange waves and disappears among the curly hair on his chest. Oh, how nice he is. She had been sure of it, she guessed it when he stood in front of her in the restaurant:—his entire body is brown, clean and muscular.

He puts his arms under her neck and looks smilingly at her. "You always ought to be naked. You are natural that way. You should never do anything other than love and be loved."

She laughs a little. "Then I would be worn out too soon. No one can last like that."

But she thinks with relief that he likes her—just like that, just as she is. She throws herself on his stomach and looks at this man lying stretched out in contentment. It is a pure animal pleasure to lie close to this man.

She strokes his smooth, tanned body with her hand, slides her hand in under his balls, puts her face against his stomach, biting gently with her lips. And she groans with pleasure. She lets her mouth glide up over his chest, tugging the fragrant hair with her teeth, on up to his arm, putting her teeth into his trembling muscles.

He lies very still, trembling, looking wonderingly at her. She laughs a little, knowing very well what he is thinking. "It's very seldom that a man is caressed like this by a girl, isn't it?"

"Yes, but how do you know that?"

"Oh, I just do."

"But, then, you are not a girl. You are the greatest, most wonderful, devilish lover of all time." His face is creased with pleasure. He raises his torso and pulls her up against him. "Where have you learned to act like this?"

"I have never really learned it—I just like it."

And she lets him pull her across his stomach, and he glides tightly and firmly into her. She bends forward, stroking her breasts caressingly against him, stretches herself backwards so that she fastens her arms around his bended knees, laughs loudly, howls aloud, from pleasure and her lust for love. Because he is wonderful, this lover of hers, and she knows that she also is wonderful, feels it in her taut body which is bubbling over with lust and pride:

What a ride of love!

A little later she jumps out of the bed. "Where is the toilet?"

"In the courtyard."

"In the courtyard? Ugh!"

He is amused by this frightened, naked girl. "Look, here is a dressing gown."

A beautiful Japanese silk kimono appears out of a drawer. Siv stands in front of the mirror, wraps the soft silk cloth around her. He has hopped back into bed, lies there and looks at her, and his voice is husky when he says, "You can keep it. It's yours. It fits you, you little doll."

She looks quickly at him and looks away again. "Thanks a lot, but I'll just borrow it, okay?" She begs him with her eyes to understand. He must not be disappointed, because things are so good as they stand between them now. She cannot accept his gift. They do not owe each other anything and must not come to do so.

He nods. "As you wish. But put it on and get it over with."

The night is beautiful. Siv stands quietly in the middle of the courtyard. She breathes the air in deeply. And the truth dawns on her, not heavily and commanding, but with a trembling bird's call at dawn: God is pleased—and the angels laugh when they watch the happy love of people.

CHAPTER FOUR

Siv is together with Lars several times a week. The black typewriter sits undisturbed beneath its dust cover. For the time being she wants only to live. She can write about life later.

She explains to him that she wants to see Copenhagen—from its exciting backside.

He straightens his back and smiles patronizingly, "That's not for you, my little doll."

"But I *want* to see it."

So he invites her to be with him and his friends and takes her out on the town. Now she is going to experience it. Now she is going to see the whole thing. She sits with a drink in front of her, smiles bravely. She's having a good time, isn't she?

She drinks until things begin to go around for her, rises from her chair, carefully but with determination, and says, "Just a minute." Then she rushes out to the toilet to throw up.

She dances with Lars in places where there is no more room than she has at home in her bathroom. People just stand there in the same spot and rub themselves against one another, getting to know each other. She visits Nyhaven, the new port, and sees thin, gray women or bloated, drunken women. She hears no spiritual talk; she only sees distorted, blubbering faces, women who come in and take their sleepy, drunken men by the arm and cry out as if they were selling fish in the marketplace.

Lars takes her by the arm. "This is no place for you, Princess."

He calls her his doll and his princess. He looks at her as if she were Cleopatra and the Virgin Mary rolled into one. She likes him, this primitive, honest seaman, makes fun of

herself and the whole show, enjoying the comedy, like a
delicate, refined woman who wants to see life as it really is.

She sees the cellars where the men go to be tattooed. It
does not hurt at all. They are too drunk to be able to
feel anything. Strange men say hello to Lars, laugh know-
ingly and admiringly when they look at Siv. He takes her
tightly by the arm and his face reddens. She smiles sweetly
and reassuringly, but a little impatiently: My God, she is
not a princess.

She goes to bars where you really cannot tell who is a
man and who is a woman there in the dark light and the
strong smell of perfume. She notices Lars' determined
hand when he drags her out of all the confusion, home to
security and love.

He is never drunk, never really drunk, her Lars. At any
rate, not when he is out with her.

He brusquely demands that she put on her coat because
of the cool night air.

She lays it demonstratively over her arm. "It's warm
out."

"It's *not* warm. Put it on. It's past two o'clock."

She still shakes her head. He takes the coat away from
her, pulls back her arms and sticks them into the sleeves
of her coat, fixes it over her shoulders with a hard tug.
"I said you were to put it on."

Her body turns warm and soft, just because of this.
She walks silently by his side, soft and tired and all
woman.

He puts his arm around her shoulders, laughs softly and
triumphantly.

But it is all right that he triumphs. He can rightfully
command. That is one of the rules of the game.

Is he aware of this? Or is he just that way?

He stops beside the wall of a house and turns toward her,
kissing her searchingly, as if he wants to find out how
soft she is. Yes, she is his woman, tonight as well.

He groans heavily and Siv knows how things really are.
That is, she understands it as an idea, but it makes no
difference. She enjoys what is going on intensely.

The whole thing is a comedy, a sweet and stimulating
comedy, because Lars is not the stronger of the two, not
in reality, but this is just a dream about reality.

He looks at her—as a woman—and nothing else.

He tramps around in his tanned, weatherbeaten skin of a sailor with slow steps and believes that women are just women.

One evening they sit across from each other in her apartment. She has bought a bottle of red wine because it is so nice to chat while drinking red wine, and Siv has made up her mind that she will also try *to be a human being* when together with Lars.

She tells him about her childhood, her background, her holy father, Svend and Heinz. She tells him just a little and very generally, looking closely at him to see if he seems to be interested, listening to see if he has a question.

But he just sits there listening to the whole thing, perhaps even looking a bit embarrassed. It is so feminine, all this talking. You just have to let them talk. He smiles reassuringly, nods reassuringly, and finally says, "Stop all this nonsense, Princess, and come over here and give me a kiss."

Siv quickly shuts the door on her strange, lonely thoughts. She smiles and gives him both her hands, walks over to him, kneels and lays her head against his abdomen, presses her neck down between his legs, feels his strong arms encircle her and settles back into her uncomplicated woman's world.

Love—nothing but love—that is a bit strange, too.

You cannot expect to find out everything all at once.

A few weeks later she visits Lars at his place. He acts differently from the way he usually does. She notices it when she comes into the dear, familiar room which smells of dust and fresh air. She does not ask any questions. She knows that she will get an explanation.

He greets her with a crooked smile, opens his hands and says, "Hello, Siv."

She likes the fact that he always greets her like this, that he does not crush and kiss her immediately, but waits until the electrical connection is in order.

There are so many things about Lars that Siv likes very much.

He walks over to a polished cabinet and opens the door

to his little bar. He is very proud of this cabinet and enjoys opening it up for his friends. "What'll you have?" He also has no problem keeping it stocked. A seaman has many connections, and they can provide him with good, but cheap, alcohol.

He does not drink very much himself and he does not smoke, simply because he does not like the taste. But he always has cigarettes for Siv and an extra pack for her to take home with her.

But now he walks over to the cabinet as soon as he sees that Siv had settled down in his big chair. Usually he does not go over to the cabinet right away, yes, sometimes it stays closed when Siv visits him and neither of them give it a thought. They do not need alcohol to find the song.

She admires his eager bent back. Lars does not wear undershirts and you can see his powerful muscles through his shirt. His sleeves are rolled up. His hard arms are strong and good. He is as healthy as an animal.

She thinks of this because he acts so differently from the way he usually does, and she wants so much to keep this healthy animal.

He turns toward her. "We'll have a drink, okay?"

"Yes, please." She looks at his eyes, steals into his mind. "A strong one." He nods gaily. "That's just what you'll get."

He comes back with two large glasses. Siv does not know what is in them, and she really does not care, but she asks just the same, "What is it?"

"Whisky and soda."

She sips and discovers: a lot of whisky and very little soda.

Whenever she has drunk whisky, she has always ended up bubbling over with good spirits. She laughs at the thought already. "I guess I'm going to be a spectacle pretty soon."

"That's for you to decide."

It sounds strange and hard. What is the matter with him?

He looks at her and throws back his head. "I was about to write to you."

"You were about to do *what?*" It sounds so incredible that Siv asks her question very loudly: He—Lars—write?

And to a girl he sees several times a week? She fastens her eyes on his hands; they are short, broad and strong. They can go around a tiller on a boat or around a girl's neck. Can they write as well?

She feels her cheeks getting warm. What is the matter?

"But you have come yourself, so the letter won't be necessary."

"What were you going to write to me about?"

She questions him very seriously, the way you question a child to find out whether he has taken his mother's purse.

"Well—yes." He sits back in his chair and takes a gulp of his whisky, bends forward and carefully sets the glass down. "Well—"

"What's up, Lars?"

"You probably think that I'm a fool?"

"No."

"You see, it was only meant to be a joke—between us."

Siv nods. Many thoughts cross her mind: What does he mean? What is he getting at? Yes, it was just a joke, a delightful, warm joke.

She says the words, "A delightful joke."

He winces a bit as if he does not like the fact that she agrees with him.

Then it bursts out of him. "I want to marry you, you know."

He says it as if it were something disgraceful over which he has no control. "You do?" Siv lowers her head. This is a compliment, a very big compliment—which she cannot accept.

"I've gotten berth on a ship to the Orient."

"Oh?" She looks at him with surprise.

He clears his throat, drinks some more, continues, "I've got to make some money. My father is well now, so my help here at home is no longer needed."

"Yes, I can very well understand that." She keeps herself from looking at him. She cannot control the look in her eyes.

"You're just the right girl for me."

Siv thinks: I'm the right girl for a lot of people. But she does not say it. She is silent.

"I remember the evening when you made me that

apple pie. I can remember so much that you have done for me which no other girl has ever done—I—I would be very proud to have you meet my father and mother." He laughs, pleased at the thought. And he looks at her so that she feels ashamed of herself.

Make an apple pie? Anybody can make an apple pie, can't they? But she had made one on a happy evening while Lars stood behind her, kissing her on the neck and slapping her behind. That apple pie was baked in the heat of love, and therefore tasted heavenly. But he believes that no one can bake them the way I can. She asks in a small voice, "Do you think we should get married now? You are going away, aren't you?"

"Yes, I'm to leave in three weeks."

That's one difficulty. What is she supposed to say? That she does not love him? No, that would be too evil.

She cannot answer, just sits with a lowered head.

He leans over and grabs her thin, girlish arm. "What the hell, you can give me an answer, can't you?"

Yes, she must, she must. She raises her head and looks inploringly at him. "I can't, Lars. Not if you are going away." She seizes upon her own words. She can use them. "No, not if you are going away, Lars. I'm not the type who can get along without a man for so long. You know very well what kind of a person I am, don't you?"

She snuggles down into the armchair and makes herself small and helpless, childish and unhappy, opening her arms, shrugging her shoulders. "You know what kind of a person I am. I can't do without a man for a very long time."

Now he can beat her and call her a slut and a whore. Here is his chance to think that she is not worth his love. Believe it, Lars. Look at it that way. That is the easiest way to look at it.

But Lars does not let himself be fooled. He understands the reason or feels it. "Well, this is the last time we'll be together, then."

He says it so coldly, tightening his mouth; his eyes become hard and antagonistic.

Siv opens her mouth, closes it again without saying a word. Didn't he say that he wouldn't be leaving for three weeks? Very well, since he thinks that this is to be the last time, it's really *going to be* the last time.

She puts down her glass. It is empty and has not made her cry. She stretches her arms and put them softly and lazily around his neck, blinking her eyes to keep back her tears, and whispers caressingly, "Okay. Give me a drink."

They drink a lot. They drink much too much, but it does not help. They go to bed, but now there is an unwilling, brutal note in their happy song of love.

It is night. Siv slips out of his bed, looks lovingly at this healthy man, feels a desire to kiss his crooked eyebrow, does not dare because he would probably wake up. She carefully puts on her clothes, softly closes the door and disappears into the night and her loneliness.

CHAPTER FIVE

A new nurse has been assigned to her ward. When Siv is introduced to her, they discover that they already know each other. Her parents belong to the same sect as Siv's father and mother.

Siv greets her as if they had been bosom buddies. "Is it really you, Lise? Welcome."

She is a bit angry with herself. Why all this hypocrisy? She is not at all interested in Lise. But Lise stands there with a smile all over her round face. She looks like a happy, playful puppy. Siv almost expects to see her tongue stick hungrily out of her mouth. She is tall, with large breasts, long, strong legs, blonde, wavy hair which hangs softly around her oval, red cheeks. She is really very attractive, well-proportioned, but this impression is disturbed by her round, childish face. Her eyes are also round, and sky-blue. She looks like a buxom child, upholstered in the right places for playing parlor games.

Siv's next comment bursts forth, thoughtlessly and spontaneously. "How are old you now?"

Lise laughs. "I'm just as old as you, remember?"

"Oh—yes."

Siv pulls herself together. "How are your parents getting along?"

"Fine. They are now living here in Copenhagen."

The head nurse nears them. Lise straightens up, pulls back her powerful body and looks humble. Miss Svendsen gives them a friendly smile. "Oh, so you know Miss Esruth. How wonderful. She can show you around, then." She walks on and Siv takes Lise by the hand and leads her into the dressing room. When Lise has changed clothes, and they are about to go through the door, she turns toward Siv and looks at her full of expectation. "Are you getting along all right?"

"Sure, what do you think? Now that I have things just the way I want them."

"You've become awfully pretty."

Siv starts, looks questioningly at Lise, but her blue eyes do not betray her. She once more expects to see her tongue hang hungrily out of her mouth.

It does not happen.

"Can I come and visit you?"

"Sure, whenever you like." And Siv means what she says.

In the days which follow they are very often together, and never has Copenhagen seen greater opposites. They take long walks, arm in arm, sauntering and talking: a slim, dark, delicate girl with an uneasy curiosity and all the knowledge of the world in her narrow, angular face, and a large, blonde, chubby woman with round, surprised, happy eyes, strutting bravely along in a pair of slacks which reveal much too much of her big behind—with over-sized knitted jackets and blouses. She always buys them several sizes too big. She confided to Siv that she feels smaller then.

There is something touching and helpless about this light-haired woman in spite of her size and healthy looks. You do not find it surprising that she is a virgin, that she giggles and laughs at the strangest times, that she sits on the tarred railing down by the harbor so that she has to go home with a black stripe across her behind, that she is constantly on the verge of doing something wrong and yet manages to save herself in her awkward, puppy-like way.

But she can sit as still as a mouse listening to Siv's stream of talk, her opinions about life and love. She is a good listener because these things really interest her. She lives Siv's life vicariously, and Siv dishes it out with a little pang of conscience: How on earth can she bring herself to listen to all of this?

But Lise listens, and now and then she rubs her hands together, her sweet, blue eyes turning bright with enthusiasm. "Oh, Siv, how great it must be to have experienced such things!"

Siv becomes silent and ashamed of herself. Why is she sitting here making Lise long for such things? Her life is no life for Lise. But still, it really is wrong for somebody to be twenty-three years old and have never experienced sex, isn't it?

Siv has begun to make friends in Copenhagen: nurses with friends and acquaintances, Lars' friends and acquaintances, doctors who drop in on Siv for a drink and a chat. She invites Lise over together with some friends. She sits looking at the girl, at the eyes of the men, friendly, indifferent eyes, every now and then a look of amusement. She shoves them out of the door together. "You'll take Lise home, won't you?"

One of the men nods politely. "Of course I will."

The following day she sees Lise's eyes. They are upset and childishly wounded. "Nothing happened. You are the only one they are interested in."

Siv gets a lump in her throat. "You don't wear the right kind of clothes."

She goes with her into shops, makes purchases, argues, complains, "You shouldn't wear pink. You can't wear slacks. Buy yourself a tight dress and a pair of high-heeled shoes."

"I can't wear high-heeled shoes. You should just see me. I look like a waddling duck. And a tight dress? You must be out of your mind. I wouldn't be able to move my legs."

Siv looks with resignation at the happy, giggling face. "Buy what you like, then." And Lise buys a thick, red blouse, a big masculine jacket which makes her look like a broad-shouldered soldier.

Siv sighs, but gives in. Why does she want this clumsy girl to get mixed up with sex? She certainly would not be able to manage an affair.

Siv has been to Lise's home a few times, but she has not seen her parents. They have been either at prayer meeting or at work. On the other hand, she has met Lise's two younger sisters and her younger brother. Siv thinks that they are noisy and irritating. Tonight she is invited to dinner. She would prefer not to go, but does not have the heart to say no.

She is introduced to Lise's mother and is shown into the parlor. The furniture is worn and ruined in a brutal fashion. She is shoved down into an armchair by Lise, who bounces around in a way sillier than usual.

The mother walks back and forth between the parlor and the kitchen, mumbling, "What a blessing."

Siv stares secretly, wondering: "What in the world is it that this woman sees as a blessing? A mother of four spoiled children whose dirty clothes are spread all over their rooms, whose shoes stand in the bathroom, dirty and unwashed, who come rushing through the door in a gust of selfishness, whose very being and every act is but a single demand for clothes, food, room to live in and affection."

Siv looks once more at the wife. She scurries around, busy and occupied with small, unimportant things. Dorothy does not like this fork so it is exchanged for another, a thin potato fork. This chair is broken. She sits in it herself so that she can see that it does not fall to pieces, and anyway, she does not sit very much; she must see that all goes well. She smooths a crease in the tablecloth, trips out to the kitchen, tests the potatoes and turns over her beef.

The door is open and Siv looks at the red, sharp arms through the fog of steam and frying. Lise's mother has red arms, swollen, neglected hands. A large, simple, checked apron is tied solidly around her sharp hips. Her hair is gray, thin and pulled into a tight little knot at her neck. She has no time for curlers, or creams for her rough hands. She hasn't the money, and anyway, it is not necessary to have these things. She is a mother, a housewife, the slaving soul in a little man's world, home and children —large, strong children with red cheeks and grown-up shoe sizes. It costs a lot to keep them well-dressed. It is hard work polishing their muddy shoes so that the leather is not damaged, but stays nice and soft for their next trip through the muddy hills.

Siv sits and fills up with a dark anger directed at this wife, this poor, worn-out housewife, who, to her stupid self-destruction, walks around looking like a dried-out, bony rack, a robot without any claim to its own life and its own pleasures.

But the thing which she cannot understand, the most incomprehensible thing of all, is that mumbled sentence which comes out of this taut, bloodless mouth. "What a blessing!" Does she mean, maybe, that she is gathering up treasures in heaven which neither moths nor rust can destroy?

God is, for Siv, something incomprehensible, something

indescribably large and thrilling. A pressure of force, an inspiration. He is to be found in everything great. He lives in art, beauty, in ugliness and love, in sex and in all the great geniuses.

But the God who shows Himself in this half-dead wife is a strange god. He comes through her lips with a lost stubborn groan, "What a blessing!"

A blessing? A blessing to grow gray and withered for nothing? Siv thinks of Lise's father. "Does he have sex with his wife?" she wonders. He must, since they have four children. And if now, in spite of her exhaustion, she still fulfills her marriage duty, does she whisper in her heart: "What a blessing?"

Siv has sat running her nails nervously up and down the upholstery of the armchair. The others look at her with irritation. "Please stop that, Siv. It's a horrible sound."

She stops and puts her hands in her lap, sits and plays with her garter, which she has gotten hold of through her dress, letting it smack repeatedly against her thigh. She looks at the flowery, brownish wall-paper, at the smoking stand with its polished top and its clean, unused ashtrays. Why do they have a smoking stand if it is a sin to smoke?

No, she looks helplessly around. God is not here, nor is the devil. But she crosses her legs, sealing her warm, nervous sex, trying to look at these things calmly and tolerantly. What is wrong? She is the one who is crazy. This is a good bourgeois home. The mother is the model of a conscientious housewife. The children are healthy, red-cheeked and lively. Someday, when they leave this home, they will take with them a firm idea of what a home is. Yes, a home, the basic unit in a well-organized society.

If the world patterned itself after wild, restless gypsy souls like hers, there would be terrible confusion. But isn't it possible—possible to have the best of both worlds? Both protect one's children and love life?

You silent, brave army of gray, worn-out women. Would anything happen, would you lose anything, if you did not forget the beauty of things?

What if you let your children go to school one day with unpolished shoes because you did not have time to polish them? Because you had taken a warm bath in bath salts, because you had made your body soft and clean for the father of your children?

Would you lose anything if you closed the door of your children's room one evening: "You've got to play by yourselves. Mommy and Daddy are not to be disturbed."

What if you then walked over to your husband, your comrade in the difficult art of living, stroked your lips against his neck and let your hands slide down between his legs. If you later came in to your children, taking them by the cheeks and kissing them good night, smelling of warm sex. What would you have lost, you little gray wife?

Oh, yes. The children have to be looked after, they come first. You have to see that they wash themselves properly and put their clothes neatly away. When you have gone into the parlor, they cry out that they want a glass of water or that their blanket has fallen off.

They finally fall asleep, but you have to sew a couple of hooks on your oldest daughter's skirt and hang a pair of stockings up to dry.

Your husband reads the newspaper. It is time for coffee. You get up with a groan, walk out and put on the coffee and fix the tray. You will now have your coffee and then go to bed to sleep. You are tired. You have rushed back and forth the whole day. The husband and wife talk a little together while they drink their evening coffee, but then they have to hear the news report; they cannot miss that.

The husband stands up, stretches and yawns, winds up the clock and goes out to lock the door. You take out the cups and look in at the children for the last time.

Then you are in bed. Perhaps your husband reaches over and pulls you to him. You raise your hand and put out the light, turning your face away because he has thrown his socks by the side of the bed and they smell strongly of sweat. He knows that his socks stink, because you have told him so, but he cannot be bothered with that. You are just his wife and not a strange, exciting mistress.

Yes, just his wife. She has an acid smell because she is too tired to wash herself before going to bed.

You are together in an even rhythm for five minutes.

After a while you say sleepily, "Remember to pay the telephone bill tomorrow. It's the last day."

He growls a little and turns his back on you.

And the bedroom grows silent with heavy sleep.

Siv sits at the table with her hands folded. Grace is being said. The man of the house is not at home, but the wife prays in her husband's spirit. "As a matter of fact, she prays constantly," said Lise when Siv asked about her mother's mumbling. "You see," Lise had explained, "my mother lives in her own world with God. She walks around the whole time praying to Him. It gives her strength, or so she says." This "or so she says" came out so slowly, so helplessly full of doubt, that it seemed to Siv as though Lise had some idea that it would have been better for all concerned if her mother said, "Satan."

Lise's mother says the grace in a crisp, trembling voice. Siv looks openly at her. It does not matter, because the rest of the family sits with bowed heads, and Lise's mother has closed her eyes as she prays. The closed eyelids are white, the eyelashes short and light and her cheeks are bluish with broken blood vessels. A little spot on each jaw is red and swollen from agitated nerves.

Siv feels a trembling restlessness in her hands, and she wants to let out a resounding curse into the little room. She thinks of her own home, of her chubby mother, healthy and round, and of her fanatically burning father.

They are also "saints." They belong to the same sect as Lise's father and mother, but just the same, there is a difference. In her home there has never been this starnge, doomed atmosphere of dying life. And her father had been responsible for that—her father, who is such a sensual, loving Christian.

She sits picking at her food, longing to be home with the man who prays a hard-won, humble thanks to God and, afterwards, throws himself into his food like a starving animal.

And her mother was warm because her father burned. Her mother was a Christian because her father was a fanatic in his belief. A warm, naïve, protected hen who hid herself under her husband's personality and strength.

Siv sits there and is deeply ashamed of her earlier criticism of her home. Compared to this house of prayer, her home has been a festive castle, correct in all its wasted belief in God. Because people *lived* there.

When she is to leave, Lise shows her to the door. "You didn't like Mother, did you?"

Siv looks nervously and closely at Lise's face.

"No, I didn't."

Lise laughs. "No, I could tell. You sat so uneasily."

They talk no more of that. It is never necessary to give lengthy explanations to Lise. She accepts Lise in the same way that she accepts her existence: incomprehensible, comic, nothing to be concerned about.

CHAPTER SIX

There is a washroom on the hall of the surgery ward where the doctors stand and wash themselves "sterile." Two doctors are there now: a very young intern whom Siv does not know and the first assistant doctor who has been on her ward for a month and with whom she has become acquainted. Yes, Siv has begun to get to know him, and is glad.

He is tall, a little sway-backed, has dark red, bristling hair, a long, sharp nose, blue-green eyes which shine and change expression. And deep lines or grooves run from his eyes up toward his forehead which remind Siv of a drawing of Mephistopheles. He looks like a husky, alarming mountain.

She examines herself in the mirror which hangs on the wall beside the telephone: Is she pretty today? Are her eyes shiny and clear, and her skin clean? Does her apron hang from her hips the way it should? She rubs away a shiny spot under one of her eyes. Yes, it'll do. She is just as pretty as she usually is.

She turns and looks at Doctor Dam, who has walked over to the shiny containers which hold sterilized white coats. He nods toward the containers, and she hurries over to open the lid so that he can take out a towel with his clean hands. He dries himself, throws the towel on the floor, picks up a white coat and sticks his arms in it. In the meantime he looks at Siv, and she feels that he smiles behind his mask. It is also annoying that he saw her looking in the mirror. She steps back a little so that he will have room to turn around. He now stands with his back to her. He is to be buttoned and tied up behind. She will have to stand up on her toes in order to reach the top buttons.

Yes, here is the doctor, tense already, no doubt, concentrating on the coming operation. He has spoken to the patient who has confidently placed himself in his hands. He has studied the charts and pondered over the best way to make this particular incision. It is important. It concerns a human being, a sleeping but living organism of flesh and blood, soul and senses. Siv knows that this is the way this doctor looks at the matter. That is why she respects him. What kind of a human being are you if you have no respect for life?

And yet! When she is behind him and has to stand on her toes to reach the top buttons, when she fumbles nervously and clumsily: His neck is so broad and strong.

She gets angry with herself. Will I never change? I, a nurse, who should be nothing but a nurse at this moment, a good, calm and serious helper. Well, well, she comforts herself at once, it could just happen that he is just like her—behind his mask.

She ties his sash. He mumbles, "Not so tight."

She loosens it a bit and lightly nudges him. "There you are."

And he turns around and looks down into her dark, all too talkative eyes, and she can see now that he is smiling. His eyes are drawn out into thin lines. "Thanks."

They walk into the operating room. The operation can begin.

And when the bright light is turned on, when everything is a sharp white and green, when all hands are covered by brown rubber gloves and the table stands prepared with the various instruments, it is then that Siv can manage to forget herself; it is then that she is adequate—as a nurse.

The entire world is compressed into a small sphere with a single focal point. She hands out instruments, washes, dries, almost not hearing the short orders, because her eyes are fastened on the open wound, surrounded by shiny forceps. She knows what is needed before the words are said.

It is not dreadful to work in an operating room. It is not upsetting and queasy. It is a hypnotizing, tense concentration of all one's powers. It is holy and good and close to life itself.

She feels the perfect assurance which lives in the doctor's hands. She learns his rhythm and technique.

These are happy hours.

But when Doctor Dam is not performing an operation, he does not seem to be a strict and serious surgeon.

There is something impish, something slouchy about his long body when he comes sauntering across the corridor. His eyes are happy and playful, and his pale mephistophelian face shines with a sarcastic humor.

Siv slips out into the hall when she hears his voice. She trips away looking occupied. She walks into the supply room, looking around—is there anything she needs? She takes a container of cannulae—she has to have something when she goes out. She walks slowly back across the hall, almost grazing him, and is happy when she captures his smile and eyes. It also happens that he stops her and asks her about one thing or another. And the day she realizes that he had asked her about something quite trivial just to have her stop, yes, that day Siv begins to have new dreams. She takes very good care of her skin, buys her own wooden shoes because the hospital's are much too big and clumsy. She wears her apron more tightly, walks gracefully and erect when she sees the ugly devil, whose face would be a joy for a caricaturist. She makes fun of herself because she never has anything else on her mind but men. She tells herself that she is a stupid, sluttish, superficial young girl, whose heart starts beating at the sight of a white coat. But these silent reprimands do not help. The woman in her leaps up whenever she sees Eric Dam. And this woman bursts through her skin and eyes, through her walk and movements, through her smile and voice. It bursts out through the nurse who should be thinking only about patients, illnesses and cures while at the hospital.

But she is good to herself, this Siv. She knows how to find excuses. She treats herself the way a mother treats a difficult child: Others do the same, don't they? It isn't just her. It can't be, can it? Perhaps the others hide it better than she can. She looks suspiciously at her sister nurses, examining their faces when they talk to Eric Dam. They also stand up on their toes. They also smile differently from the way they usually do. She calmly flounces on. She is not the only one who thinks that he is wonderful, but, but she would prefer him to think that *she* is the only one who is wonderful.

He addresses all the nurses, young and old alike, with a good-natured, "Yes, my sweet, yes, Miss————." And if it is busy in the hall, if it is difficult to find a doctor willing to spare a few minutes for a minor detail, they usually ask Doctor Dam if he wouldn't . . . ?

He almost always says yes, but it *can* happen that he raises an eyebrow, glances sceptically at the imploring look and the engaging touch on the arm.

"No, Miss————, you'll have to find someone else to-day."

He is just as stubborn as he is good-natured. You let him go with a sigh and see if you can find another doctor.

It is a known fact that old men have difficulty passing their water. Eric Dam is an angel when he helps old men whose prostate has become tight or closed. A big, square, hairy angel with an impressive, incomprehensible interest in the sorrowful remains of an old, trembling male, whose greatest, last and only worry is to be able to urinate.

The patients are wheeled into him in a special room fitted especially for this illness and its treatment.

It is best to close the door to this room when Eric Dam is busy with his examinations. It is best to close it tightly.

Old men are often half-deaf. Nor are they very quick to understand what they are told, and if the door is not closed, you can hear unusual yells and requests from the room.

At first he speaks quietly and politely to them. They are to do this and that. When he tells them to, they are to press.

"What?"

"Yes, when I tell you to, you are to press."

"Oh, am I?" The old man nods willingly and confidently and sends a stream up over the doctor's apron.

He changes, sits patiently down again and starts all over. "Not before I tell you to, Mr. Henriksen. Remember that this time."

Now the old man is completely aghast. It was terrible

that he soiled the doctor. He must be more careful.

Then the doctor is ready. *"Now,* Mr. Henriksen, press."

"What?"

"You can press now."

But the man lies there twisting. "What?"

And then Eric Dam starts yelling. And it is then that it is good to have the door closed so that the patients waiting outside for their turn will not be inhibited by fear. They are already quite nervous as it is.

"Piss, old man! Piss like hell! Piss like the devil!"

A little while later you might hear: "Well, old chap, now you are just as good as new."

Siv stands behind the door shaking with laughter. She dries the tears from her eyes, fixes the patient's covers and wheels him out into the hall, comes back into the room again, where she meets the doctor's bright eyes and mischievous smile.

She is on the verge of falling seriously in love.

It is three o'clock in the afternoon. Doctor Dam has had a lot of patients today. She looks tiredly around at tubes, connections, dirty instruments and capsules. She has to clean up once more, but it has been a wonderful day and it has become a fast rule that Siv assists in this room. It is a special room in which she has assisted so often that she has learned a regular routine. The head nurse assigns her to this room whenever there is a patient for Doctor Dam. Could he have said something about preferring her, because she is familiar with his methods? Or is it something which has just happened all by itself? All the same, it is wonderful.

What is she going to do in the evening? She does not want to be alone. Her body is restless and needs somebody. She does not want to write. Perhaps there is a film in town worth seeing? She will ask Lise if she wants to go along. "What does Eric Dam do in the evenings?" she wonders.

Oh, he is sure to have many friends and girl friends and interests which she knows nothing about.

The door opens behind her and Eric Dam walks in.

He walks over and stands against the wall by the desk. "Miss Esruth, we didn't finish writing the last report."

She takes the day book he hands her, sits down at the desk, with her pen ready.

"Yes?"

He raises his eyebrows, sighs, dictates and comes to a standstill.

She waits a little, looks up. "Yes?"

"Yes, yes." He says it impatiently and stands lightly hitting the wall with his hands. They look as if they are too large for his narrow wrists, and he clenches them as if they need something to take hold of.

Siv is surprised. He must be angry? But he has no reason to be angry. She is sitting there with her pen ready and is waiting for his wise words, isn't she? She looks at him and gets warm in her clothes. She senses what is the matter, but does not dare believe it.

He lets go of the wall and paces back and forth, mumbling, "Yes." Then he stops abruptly behind her. "You said: 'Yes, yes, yes'—do you always say that?"

She does not answer, but nervously moves her toes in her wooden shoes.

He laughs a little, walks up close behind her and puts his hands on her breasts. Then he says slowly and with emphasis, "Say 'yes' once more—can I fuck you?"

Siv's body turns stiff with wonder, not at his question, but at the words he uses.

She twists herself free, turns and looks searchingly up at him. She has to say no the first time. Of course, she must say no! That is what you always say.

She shakes her head with determination and looks down.

He puts one of his hands on her shoulder, supports the other against the wall and looks at her with a warm smile. "Nonsense!"

She wrinkles her brow and tries to look angry and decent. She does not succeed very well, because this man really means it, really means what he says. She feels a cry of hurrah inside her. Her insides sing yes and amen.

Because what else does a man say to a girl?

"Can I make love to you?" Or preferably, "I want to make love to you."

But you love with the heart. That is nothing which you can decide to do in the next few hours.

Oh, how often has Siv pondered over the wrong words,

and there now rushes through her brain a storm of thoughts:

You can love animals, children, the truth, beauty, music, sex, art—life. You can also love another person, and it can happen that you can love with your heart and fuck with your body at the same time—and then everything is perfect. Then the indescribable happens, that which is so strangely great and true and which a person experiences very seldom.

But when a strange man asks a woman if he can make love to her, it sounds wrong and stupid. He does not really mean *love*.

What else is said to a girl? "Can I go to bed with you— I *want* to go to bed with you!" But that is not correct either, because it does not always happen in bed. It can happen anywhere people can be alone with each other. "I want to sleep with you." That is even less appropriate.

"I have to have you!" That is also said sometimes. But this is nonsense. People can never *have* each other. You can do something together, but no one has really ever owned another.

Yes, Siv has thought of all of this, and she has also thought of what others would say if she tried to explain it.

Because if you say it right out, where is the romance?

But that which most people call romance is, in Siv's eyes, a false, deceptive thing. She finds it in the silence between two people who understand each other; she does not find it in words. If no words are needed, then everything is perfect. But if words have to be used, then make sure that you use the right words.

Why don't we use the correct words?

Because these words have been demeaned through the ages by people with bad consciences.

There is a verse lacking in the Bible. It should read: "Unless ye become as the animals, ye shall never enter the kingdom of heaven."

That is the way it has to be. We are holy animals with brains, and every now and then we have to forget our brains and be humble and thankful that we are also created like animals. Siv sees this as her truth, and she has shrugged her shoulders when men have propositioned her incorrectly, because they thought it was necessary for them to do so: You have to act like a well-brought up person, with girls, at any rate.

But a language is poor if it has no word for one of the most important things in life.

Shame on you, you Danish dictionary. Shame on all you nations that deny these words admittance. For they exist, but must not be used.

People whisper "fuck," "cunt" and "prick" with a dirty, lurid smile.

And the animal in them cries, sobs, mocks, fights and grinds its way out with a distorted face, with a mean snicker.

They are ashamed that God has created them as animals.

Yes, Siv has these completely insane ideas inside her, and the strange thing is that she really believes them.

She boldly and frankly asks God to be her witness. She never feels Him to be closer than when she, heavy with expectation, walks toward the waiting embrace of a man.

If it were up to her, then all the sweet literature from the romantic age, about sheiks and pursued, screaming women who didn't enjoy it, about the scent of flowers from the skin of virgins, about the glorification of untouched virtue—all this would be gathered off bookshelves.

She would have it all burned in a powerful auto-da-fé—as a tribute to the woman who does not smell of flowers but of her own longing juices—as a tribute to the man who dares to fuck without calling it "loving" and to the woman who dares to say "yes" instead of "shame."

We should learn to fuck like animals and love like God.

All this rushes through Siv's brain in the course of a few seconds as she sits with Eric Dam's hand on her shoulder, because she has often thought these thoughts before. And her truth is now confirmed by this tall, bent, smiling man who asks so strongly and well: "Can I fuck you?"

She smiles a little. It is impossible for her to say anything.

Because whenever a man asks this in the right way, he deserves a yes—and perhaps deserves to be *loved* as well.

He shakes his head lightly. "I can, can't I?"

"Yes," she manages to whisper, "yes, you can."

She turns her head and brushes her chin against his

hand, looks up at him with a sparkling smile and says loudly and clearly, *"Yes, you can."*

He laughs. "Can I come by this evening?"

"Yes."

She should have been upset by the terrible words. She should have waited a week before giving her consent, yes, letting the man walk around in hope and fear.

But no, it is too wonderful, and she has desired him for so long, this pale devil with his red hair.

He lets go of her, and she walks over to the basin and begins to dismantle the instruments. They have lain too long in blood and dirt and are difficult to take apart.

He walks over and helps her. "Please let me, Siv."

She hears the texture of his voice. It is new and husky, and she now knows that it did not matter that she gave in at once.

He walks toward the door. "This evening at eight o'clock?"

The rest of the day is nothing, nothing, nothing.

She changes the linen on the beds. She laughs so that her sister nurses laugh, too. She fusses with the covers of trays that are to be put into the sterilizer. She puts away clothing, sterilizes hypodermics and needles, cleans cannulae. Her hands do this, her eyes watch, her mouth laughs and talks.

Just walk around and talk, just laugh, bounce and trip —get it over—over.

Home to the apartment, into the bathtub, let her hands glide over her body, spray perfume behind her ears and between her legs, brush her hair, walk back and forth in the room until it is eight o'clock. Nothing to eat, because her throat is dry and tight with expectation.

A woman never lives so intensely as in the hours before she is to meet a man whom she is to experience for the first time.

She is so happy that her skin contracts in a trembling fright. She is so warm that she has to unbutton the top of her dress.

This is the happiest, the greatest, the most wonderful thing that exists, because in such hours you are not normal, and you think that you have a right to be happily insane.

She puts her elbows on the windowsill, looks out into

the street and sighs, "Oh." She turns around for herself in front of the mirror and sighs, "Oh."

What is it? Did she want to go to Egypt? Did she want to become a famous writer? There was also something about a dress that she had looked at several times and wanted to buy, but did not have the money.

What does all this mean? Clothes, food, money, travel? What does it mean, when Eric Dam is coming this evening and is to be her lover?

CHAPTER SEVEN

But Lise? She still does not have a lover, does she?

Siv has a bad conscience because of Lise. She really has no reason to have one. But it is a great shame that Siv feels so happy now.

Her happiness shines out of her eyes, her voice and her smile. She is unable to hide it from anybody, not even from Lise. She cannot help telling her how happy she is.

Lise should be happy as well. Everybody should be happy. But is Lise really unhappy? No. She is obviously not. She laughs and looks at Siv with curiosity, and bounces across the hall with a little extra silliness. But her blue eyes do not take part in her laughter. They look at Siv questioningly and with wonder. They are confused somewhat and perhaps a bit sad: Why can't she also—?

But one morning when they meet each other on the ward, she looks at Siv with a silly, strange glance. Her ruddy cheeks are a bit swollen and her eyes are blurred.

Siv looks at Lise often during the course of the day, but they are both very busy and have no time for private conversation.

She tugs Siv's arm during the lunch break. "I'll come by this evening if you are not expecting a visit from Eric. I've got something to tell you."

Siv decides that it must be some good news because Lise looks insanely happy. She whispers teasingly, "Have you been together with a man?"

"Yes."

Siv jumps. She said yes, didn't she?

And she now takes back all the love she had wished for Lise. She can find no rational reason for it, but she has a feeling that Lise has done something stupid, something fatally stupid. But, so what? She has done stupid things as well, hasn't she? But Lise? She is different, and things cannot have happened the way they should have.

She hears the whole story in the evening.

Lise comes bouncing in as usual. She sits down on Siv's sofa in such a way that her feet are off the floor before she lands on her seat. The sofa creaks and groans, and for once Siv is irritated. Can't she be more graceful? She has on large boots. She kicks them across the floor, gets up and puts them together. She pulls off her socks, turns to the window and hangs them outside with a clip. She turns toward Siv while doing this and says with a laugh, "They've got to be aired. They smell of sweaty feet."

Then she flounces down again on the sofa and looks at Siv, who is faint with irritation. She really does not know why, because Lise is always like this and she usually does not get upset because of her. But she is a woman now, at least she says so, and a woman does not act like this. She carries on like a clumsy adolescent boy.

Can she be completely normal? she wonders. "Well, tell me then."

Siv bites her lips and senses her irony. Her voice had been sharp and anxious as a nervous mother's.

Lise leans back in the sofa, pulls her legs up under her and shakes her soft, blonde hair. "Yes."

She had met a man. He had visited her home.

Her home?

Yes, he was a friend of her mother's who had come with a message. He had eaten with them. He was from the country and wanted to see the town. Lise had offered to go out with him.

How old was he?

Oh, in his mid-thirties. He was so nice and had been very kind. He had taken her to a lot of small, funny places which she had never thought existed. He had a car—an Opel Captain—blue.

Lise's mouth is round with excitement when she says "blue."

"Go on."

"We drove outside of town."

"Yes?"

"We got out and took a walk in the woods."

"And that's where it happened?"

"Yes."

"Were you drunk?"

"No, not really. I was in very good spirits, though. And we had no difficulty talking with each other. He was—he was—very nice."

"But the other thing, was that nice?"

"Yes. I think so."

"Hmm."

Siv is sitting in her chair, like a tailor, with her hands holding tightly onto her toes. It helps her keep her body still. She feels an incomprehensible fear for Lise. She must not show it. No, how could she show it? She, who has told this person about love, she, who has explained to her how valid and good it is.

She smiles faintly at Lise's expectant face. (Little Lise, you are not like me. You are a child. Oh, why are we so damned selfish that we always have to try to push off our ideas on others, to fill them up to the brim with something they cannot understand?)

But it would have happened just the same, wouldn't it? Of course, it would have happened, sooner or later—and why not? It is normal, isn't it?

But Siv suddenly understands her fear: Lise is *not* normal.

She asks carefully, "Were you careful?"

"No." This is said quite cheerfully, as if you had asked her whether she had washed her hands.

"Was he?"

"I don't know." Lise wrinkles her brow. "I don't think so."

Siv gets furious. "Well, you're probably pregnant, you know, and it doesn't surprise me. Yes, it is sure to turn out wrong. I just can't make you out, a grown-up nurse."

Lise's alarmed face causes her to stop. She goes over and sits beside her on the sofa and puts her arms around her. "The whole thing is just great. I envy you. Are you going to see him again?"

"Yes." Lise nods with relief. "He's coming to town again next month and we'll go out again."

"Is he married?"

"No, and he must have a very good job—with a car like that, and all the money he spent on me."

"Well, then, you've got something to look forward to."

"Yes," says Lise. "Yes." And she bounces up and down on the sofa. "Yes." Her whole, dear, foolish, apple-like face was one big smile.

But Siv sits there with tears in her throat and does not know why.

CHAPTER EIGHT

Siv forgets her worries about Lise. She has become Eric Dam's mistress, and they are together in hot and violent sex, together in a quiet, intimate friendship.

Eric is an enthusiastic fisherman. They go off on week-end trips in his car with an old, narrow tent, a smelly kerosene burner and cans of food.

He eats with her, sleeps with her—and she is madly in love. She never gets tired of looking at his face: his happy, strong eyes with their flitting, red, bushy eyebrows that look as if they had been put on by a beautician, his amusing, grooved, devilish forehead, yes, the whole of his long, angular, loose-jointed body, with its unusually thick neck on his slightly rounded shoulders.

He looks like some thoughtless whim of the Lord, a charming mixture of accidentals.

It is Saturday evening. Siv and Eric are at a lake in the forests of Nordsjælland, north of Copenhagen. He stands at the edge of the lake trying to catch something for supper. Siv lies on a rise, with her arms behind her neck. The sun has gone down; the bushes behind the two of them have gotten dark.

She sneezes.

He turns around and looks at her. "You mustn't lie there and freeze."

"I'm not freezing."

"You've got to be. You have almost nothing on."

No, she hasn't. Just shorts and a shirt, which is open far down her breasts.

"Go over there and put on some clothes."

Just because he is ten years older than she, he doesn't have to treat her like a child. "No, I don't want to."

She can tell from his neck that he is tightening his

mouth. He likes, and at the same time does not like, her when she acts like this.

"Stop fishing. You're not going to catch anything anyhow. I can open up a can of something."

"Wait a little while."

"No." She picks up a rock and throws it out into the water near his fishing line.

"I hope you're not thinking of doing that again?"

His voice is calm, but irritated.

Siv sneezes.

"Go put on some clothes."

"No."

Something in her voice causes him to turn around.

She has completely unbuttoned her blouse. Her breasts shine white against her darker skin. She is shameless, so glowing that he has to smile. "You exhibitionist, you." Then he turns back to his fishing rod. He will decide— when, where, and how.

A new rock hits the line.

He quickly reels in and turns around.

Siv jumps up.

He stands for a moment and waits, looking at the girl with the long hair and the mad eyes.

He reaches her by the bushes, grabs her by the arm, finds a switch, and Siv feels a burning blow. They tumble around in the prickly bushes and withered leaves. Silent and out of breath, they lie there looking at each other, and something bursts inside of Siv. She laughs up into his green, shiny eyes, groans, laughs out with tears streaming down her cheeks, "I love you."

Lise does not see any more of the man who took her out—and she is pregnant. One evening she sits once again in Siv's room. She has brought some records with her which she wants to play, a blaring brass combo with biting dissonances and bleating refrains, the kind of music Siv hates. Siv does not bother to remember the titles, but just waits until Lise has played them all. Afterwards, there is a welcome silence in the room.

"Well, how are things?"

"Fine."

Lise is happy and exalted. "You know, it's just great

that I'm going to have a baby, don't you agree? Yes, it's strange, but I can't bring myself to be sorry."

Lise's stomach has gotten thick and her cheeks are thin.

She has not listened to Siv's eager requests to get rid of it before it was too late. She bounces as excitely as before on the sofa. "No, Siv, it's just great."

She looks like a child who wants a doll for Christmas and knows that she will get it.

"You have to look at the purely practical side of the matter, Lise. Where are you going to have the child? And what about afterwards? Have you reserved a place in a home for infants for the baby? You'll have to work—afterwards as well."

"Oh, things will work out." And with a giggling joy, she holds up a pair of small pants to Siv. "Aren't they sweet?"

My Lord, yes. They are sweet.

After seven months have passed, she has a miscarriage and gives birth to a dead girl.

Siv visits her in the maternity ward.

She almost does not recognize her. The face which was so excited before is now colorless and lifeless. Her eyes are tired and pale.

She had thought that she would explain to Lise that, in spite of everything, this was for the best, the most practical solution. But she is unable to do so.

She looks at the girl who has been robbed of her Christmas present. She thinks of a suitcase full of small vests and pants, each article laid away with an enthusiastic sigh. She sees that Lise is no longer a child. Neither is she an adult. She is nothing.

But she pulls through and starts working again on the ward. Everyone is sweet, kind, and considerate, and gives her easier work to do.

And it is said that she is improving. She gets color back in her cheeks.

But when Siv is with her, it can happen that she suddenly begins to talk, exaltedly and with red cheeks. She talks about God, about her home, about sin and damnation, grace and forgiveness.

Siv sadly shakes her head. "You haven't committed any

sin. It is not a punishment from God that things happened the way they did. Stop this, Lise, or I'll go crazy."

"But, Siv, I knew all this when I was a child. I have now learned that the wages of sin is death. I think—I think that something terrible is going to happen to me one day."

Siv feels a shivering uneasiness down her spine and walks quickly over to the radio and turns it on. Lise's eyes had been frightened and tortured.

"Perhaps this is God's way of speaking to me. Perhaps I'll go back to Him, telling others how things worked out for *me*."

Siv jumps up, losing control of herself. "Stop this, Lise! Pull yourself together!"

She is angry and waves her arms. She thinks of a happy, clumsy girl with big blue eyes which glowed with an excited spark because of the wonderful things in life.

What she sees in front of her is the result of a certain kind of home, with its folded, knotted hands, wondering, childish eyes which look at her parents' heavy faith with fear and obsession. Young people who prefer life to death, with warm blood and healthy desires, but with a crushing burden of guilt in their hearts.

Oh, God. Can You forgive all these murders of souls which are committed in Your name?

But Lise's parents have a strong hold on her. She goes with them to meetings. She falls on her knees and begs God for redemption.

Siv asks, "I never see you any more, Lise. Can't you come by and see me this evening?"

"You've Eric, you know, and I've got to go to meeting, you see—" She bends over toward Siv and looks her right in the eye. *"You know, I thought I wanted a man—but it turned out to be God!"*

Her parents thank the Lord. For the faithful everything works out for the best. Has not the Lord said: "You and your whole house shall be saved"? What does it matter that He has to subjugate His beloved child first before He can lead her on to the right path?

During an operation one day, Lise falls to the floor. They carry her out, lay her on a stretcher, are worried and helpful. The next day she is on her feet again. But she faints several times in the course of the following week. When she comes to, she is confused and cannot remember a thing. But her eyes are veiled and full of fear.

Those on the ward say that her miscarriage has damaged her mental condition.

One night she is signed into one of the hospital's wards.

She calls for Siv, calls on God, sits up in her bed, wildly disturbed, and screams. But mostly she prays. Filled with a shrieking fear, she prays to her parents' God, begging Him for forgiveness.

Siv sits by her bed the whole night. Her parents have been refused admittance. This is the hell which has been prepared for people. A more horrible thing is not to be found. At last they have to put her in a straitjacket. She wants to get out of her bed and go down to the sea.

The following day she is transferred to a mental hospital.

Siv does not have the strength to follow her. She flees home to her room, void of feelings and thoughts.

Later she visits Lise.

She meets her in the locked hall, clad in the striped clothes of an inmate. A gray apron is tied around her hips, which have become sharp and thin. And her hair, her lovely, light summer hair, is dead and unkempt. She now looks like her mother. Her cheeks are touched with blue, and her mouth is bloodless. She approaches Siv, slightly bent over, her hands held in front of her, and she rubs them bashfully together.

Siv sees in her eyes that she feels no pain. They are distant and closed to life.

Siv's voice is very hoarse when she says, "Hello, Lise."

"Hello, Siv." Her voice is veiled and tired.

The doctor's diagnosis: schizophrenia.

Siv is allowed to take her out into the garden. They sit down beside other mental patients and watch them play ball.

This has to be a bad dream. In a moment both of them will wake up, sitting across from each other in Siv's apartment, and Lise will shake her bright hair and smile with excitement.

"Is there anything you need? Can I do anything for you?"

Siv looks eagerly into her eyes and shakes her arm. "Lise, it's me, Siv. Can't you wake up?"

She sits wiping away the tears which quickly and silently drip down on her coat. "Tell me, what are you thinking about?"

The answer comes out slowly, like a sigh from another world. "I want to go down to the sea."

Yes, the sea has always been her delight as well as Siv's. This was one thing on which they were completely agreed.

Siv was content just to walk, looking at the waves, feeling the wind, smelling the salt water. But Lise wanted to sail. Her great dream had always been to have a sailboat, and she had often yelled at completely strange sailors, to Siv's great delight. She had laughed, persuaded and fussed. She had made many friends in the yacht basin. She could sit on the wharf for hours waiting for some compassionate soul to take her out. She had helped out in boat races because she was good to have in a sailboat. She was made for a boat, her weight, her big sweaters and the fresh summer hair which became so beautiful in the sun and wind.

"You want to go down to the sea?"

"Oh, yes." And there is a faint sign of life in her pale eyes.

Siv looks searchingly around and walks back into the building. She finds one of the attendants.

"May I be allowed to take Lise down to the water? She wants to see it so badly."

She sees the nurse's surprised eyes, stumbles over the words, "I'll look after her. She has always loved the sea."

"No, it's impossible."

"But what if it could help her?"

The nurse guardedly tosses her head. *"That* won't help."

Siv flares up. "What do you know about that? I'm the one who knows her best. I believe it will help her."

"It cannot be done."

Siv walks back to Lise, takes her hand to say goodbye. It is relaxed and cold. She has already forgotten her request and is indifferent toward Siv.

"Goodbye, Lise."

Siv rushes away knowing that she will never come back.

She gets off the bus before it is completely in town. She needs to feel the fresh air against her face.

Her heart is void of feelings, Lise is dead. That gray girl in the inmate's clothing was not Lise. She walks with her hands in the pockets of her coat and feels the sun on her face. It does not give much warmth at this time of March.

A horrible thought comes into her mind: "I am cold. I have no heart. I cannot feel anything."

A young man approaches her, a young man in dirty coveralls. His blue eyes look smilingly into hers as he goes past. "Why's the little Miss so angry?"

She breathes deeply, shamefully relieved. She wants to run after him, breathe in all his dirt and lick the black stripes of soot from off his face.

As a wild victory over the gray prison clothes and dead eyes.

As an insult to the witch-dance of life.

Some girls love uniforms, others tuxedos and white shirts. Siv has a weakness for coveralls—when there is a healthy man inside them. It is very important that he be dirty.

She walks on, released, shameful because she can feel something other than sorrow, because it is wonderful to come back again to life.

CHAPTER NINE

Eric has asked Siv to marry him.

She has not given him an answer, but has just said, "Let us wait a while, Eric, let us wait. There's no reason to rush, is there?"

She does not dare say yes.

Heinz, are you still married? But does she really want to marry Heinz? No, she really does not want to. She does not want to get married at all, not yet.

There is so much she has to do, see and experience. And the world, the whole world is full of men she does not know.

But she loves Eric. She likes his face, his hands. She loves him for his easy nature, his courage and his democratic opinions, for his brutal caresses which always turn into gentleness.

But he is just one man—one man?

"Let us wait a while, Eric, let us wait."

He nodded, a bit serious, a bit different from his usual way.

She had snuggled up into his arms. "We'll wait a while, okay?"

He must not be sad, must not believe that she does not love him, because she really does. But Eric will love her until she is no longer young, all men will love her.

She does not have to get married, not yet.

Not yet. She bounces down the streets in her pride. She smiles and glances in all directions.

She is light on her feet. She is not evil. She does not wish to be evil. But she is so young. Therefore she is of the opinion that she owns the whole world, all its people, all its smiles and all its love.

She tightens a wide belt around her waist and flounces away with her impudent behind. Wearing tight-fitting blouses which show the shape of her breasts, wearing low-cut blouses which show that she is delicate, not skinny.

Has she ever had any difficulty being who she is?

No, it is just easy and wonderful.

But one evening Eric comes in, sits down the way he usually does, with an arm on the back of the sofa.

He looks thoughtfully and seriously at Siv, who is sitting in the opposite corner of the sofa, happy and relaxed.

"Siv, there's something I've got to talk to you about."

She can tell from his voice that this is something serious, something very serious. She looks at her hands, takes out a cigarette, lets him light it and leans back expectantly in her corner of the sofa.

"I've knocked up another girl."

"What did you say?"

She does not think for a moment. She only feels that she is sinking, falling down from her high peak.

"Yes."

He does not say anything else.

"But so what?"

"I want to marry her. She was five months' pregnant before she told me, so we can't do anything about it. At any rate, I don't *want* to."

Siv sinks down deeply, so deeply that she sees Eric, herself and life itself from a tiny, little, tight hole.

She manages to whisper, "Why?"

"She is so young—and frightened."

"Do you love her?"

"No, I love you."

That helped a little. He loves her, but—? She cannot understand. "Why do you want to marry this other girl, then?"

He bends over, tries to explain. It is not a good explanation, not a satisfactory explanation.

Many years later Siv thinks: What a useless explanation that was!

"You don't want to get married, do you?" He waits a while, looking expectantly at her, at this silent girl who has completely lost her ability to think. "You don't want to, do you?"

She shakes her head, she continues to shake her head,

because she cannot say anything. Her throat is thick and strange.

But he is right: She does not want to—she won't. And a painful thought bores itself into her: "Why won't I? Yes, why don't I want to? If all of this didn't exist. If he didn't sit there telling me that he wanted to marry somebody else. If I could do it all over again—would I say yes?"

She knows that she would not have, but why not? Doesn't she love him? Yes.

She sits completely still and takes an inventory of herself.

Fortunately Eric is silent, allowing her to think in peace.

I walk the streets, tired and content after my lover's embrace, looking forward to the next time, glad that I have one, one particular lover, that I do not need to do without anything—and yet?

I look at every single man to see if he looks at me. I can see at once if his eyes are alert and gleaming. I notice at once whether he is a man, whether he is contemptible or all right, whether he has courage or is afraid, and I secretly desire—I secretly desire every single man who understands my femininity.

Yes—oh, God, that is the way it is.

All those years I was together with Svend, I let myself be raped by all eyes—and enjoyed it.

I walked along with Heinz's hand on my shoulder and stole enjoyment from the glances of others.

I sat in restaurants with Lars and cast my eyes around looking for homage—homage—and was happy if I encountered a pair of strong, strange eyes.

I have gone along all my life with a tenseness in my body, a song in my blood—for all men.

I lie, soft and gentle, in my lover's arms. He looks at me and is happy that I am *his* woman. I let him keep his belief.

A man said to me one day, "If a man understands how to love a woman, then it doesn't really matter what else he has to offer."

He was a stupid man. He had learned to grab a girl around her neck and say, "I want to." But otherwise he knew nothing.

Because that is not the way things are.

Yes, all you men who shrug your shoulders and think that a woman is a mystery. She is just that, but most of all to herself.

If I am going to a party, I dress up as if I were out to win first prize in a beauty contest. I brush my hair. With my head at an angle I look into the mirror from all points of view, smiling to myself: Everyone thinks that I am lovely, don't they?

I carefully wipe my lips on three tissues, because perhaps a man will give me a kiss and the color must not rub off. I also want to be beautiful afterwards, for others to see me.

I look down my legs to see if my stockings are on right, admiring my slender legs, hoping that others will also see that they are beautiful. I stretch my whole body and laugh victoriously. I am slender and fine, elegant and fine. I enjoy looking at others' thick legs and clumsy gait because it only accentuates my own gracefulness.

I am dreadful, completely horrible. Are other women also like this, or is it just me?

And now you are sitting here, Eric—my lover for today —and are sad because you must make me sad.

Don't I have a heart? Am I just vain?

No, things can't be that bad. I possess gentleness, perhaps more than most. I can also cry and feel my sorrow.

And I can love.

Heinz, I love you, your wisdom and your experienced hands.

Lars, I love you, too. You healthy seaman who took me with a weatherbeaten smile.

And Eric—I love you, too. You know it, don't you? I love you so much that it can't be measured. I love all men so much that it can't be measured, those I have known, those I know and those I may come to know.

I love the entire male sex if only they are strong enough for me, if they know my song and can sing a harmonious duet.

I want to be allowed to love you all, to be allowed to love throughout my life. I want to embrace you all with my heart and my senses. I want to dance my dance of love before all your eyes and before the lust of the whole world.

I have paid for my ticket, paid my price.

I have paid for it with my loneliness.

Because I have always been alone. A gypsy girl is always alone. She cannot find anyone who is hers. But she finds many who want to share her loneliness and there are people with whom it is good to be lonely.

We meet each other as strangers on a train ride, in open trust. Because we don't know each other's name and won't get off the train at the same place.

I do not want to change. I cannot, because I have to follow the rhythm in my brain and in my senses, or I'll be a hypocrite.

One day we shall all be old.

Then, others will gather together their children, grandchildren, relatives and friends and know that they have been loved, *are* loved.

But I, who have been envied by many, I, who have been a threat to married women and a danger to sensible men, I, who have made a heavenly, blessed mess out of existence—I must die alone, not envied by a soul. I must die without rustling documents which lie in a drawer binding people together, die without golden rings and promises of eternal love.

Bless me, despise me, do what you will—I cannot help myself.

"Why do you want to marry her if you don't love her?"

"I've already told you why. She is so young and frightened."

(Aren't we all—frightened?)

"Do you think that you'll be able to stand it very long?"

"She's a sweet girl."

She's sweet, is she? Oh, she's sweet, is she?

Siv does not ask who the girl is, nor what she looks like.

She is sweet and she wants to get married. She will surely be a good mother, a good wife. She will look adoringly up at the rugged mountain which Siv has climbed with a triumphant cry. She will prepare his favorite dishes and find his slippers when he comes home tired in the evenings.

Siv says a good deal, but she only says it in her thoughts:

Eric, I'm also sentimental, damned sentimental, and I love my father. And some place or other in my innermost being there is always a sobbing question about this man.

Because we betray each other. Sooner or later we betray

each other or else we betray ourselves.

She says aloud, "Well, you've got to start thinking about her, don't you?"

"Yes, I do."

"And she likes you?"

"Yes, she says that she loves me."

Siv looks at Eric's hands as if she sees them for the first time. They can strike, but they can also grab carefully. They will be used only carefully on this unknown woman. She shivers and feels somewhat relieved. She would not want to be in this woman's shoes.

She raises her head and asks triumphantly, "This is goodbye, then?"

"Yes, I guess it is."

He can still be reached. She notices that he can still be reached. She hears the tense interrogative in the tossed-off words.

But does she want to reach him? Isn't it better that she be noble and great?

"I don't want to be in the way, so we'll have to stop seeing each other."

But he desires her. She notices it in the room.

Exactly like Lars, who thought that no one else could bake apple pie. Exactly like Heinz, who considered her to be an exotic animal.

She senses him in her arms and legs, feels his desire like a burning stream in her blood, senses his thoughts like a bleeding sore.

And she turns the palms of her hands up in a thoughtless, giving gesture.

He must have her—now. Everybody must have her.

He says slowly, "You're easy to understand—and damned difficult to understand." Then he smiles, somewhat cynically. "Men will always love you. You won't be alone."

You won't be alone? This is the first untrue thing Siv has ever heard him say. But she lets him say it, stands up and walks around the room, thinking crossly: "You'll find no one else like me. And you know it, you know it."

In the next moment she is humble. Life is not like this. It is not just created for young women who know that they are delightful. It is created for togetherness and companionship, it is organized into small societies with fathers, mothers and children. Yes, life is created for these children. Life is for children, for animals, for tiny, frightened women who are pregnant. It ought to be for them.

She stands in the middle of the room and looks despairingly at Eric, feeling like a statue which people admire, notice—and walk around.

But am I not to take part in life? I, who love it so much?

Yes, she is to take part. She feels with every fiber in her body that she is to take part. She just stands there where the clamor is the loudest.

She begins to laugh, without motivation, silly and bitingly evil.

He looks at her with surprise. "What's the matter?"

"I'm just laughing."

He sees her black, shiny eyes, stands up at once and walks over to her and pulls her up against him. "Siv?" There is compassion in his eyes. Compassion?

She pushes him away, laughs again, cuttingly.

He pulls her to him and holds her tightly. "My little Siv."

She can tell by his voice that he is also suffering, that he is looking for a bright path through this departure.

And she walks away from him and slowly begins to loosen her clothes: She is his mistress. He shall remember her as his mistress. He shall remember her so that his brain will burn when he takes his little pregnant wife in his arms. She sees from his eyes that he is with her, and he also begins to take off his clothes.

She lets her long slacks fall to the rug, her thighs dark and enticing against her short, white panties.

She slips her blouse and undergarments off and rocks back and forth in front of him.

He pulls her over to the sofa and she lies down on top of him, kissing him with her tongue, teeth and lips. He shall see what she is like, find out that he has been with a slut. How she will also be allowed to be what she *is*.

She casts aside all her inhibitions and shows him with concealed triumph what she is like.

She, a gypsy girl, says goodbye.

When he has gone, she is empty, empty in her body, dry in her mouth, hoarse in her throat and burningly lonely in her soul.

Was it really that good?

CHAPTER TEN

A month later and Eric is gone.

He has been appointed head physician at a hospital in Jutland, which is a good thing both for himself and Siv.

This month has been a painful one. They saw each other every day on the ward, worked together, talked together, remembered and longed.

But Eric had not asked Siv for anything, had not asked to visit her. Siv thought every day: "Today he'll say something which will allow me to invite him home to my apartment, my sofa and me!"

She is indifferent about the other woman. She had said rather nobly: "I don't want to be in the way."

Oh, yes, she does. She wants to be in the way, because she is suffering and is evil.

A generous person? What is a generous person? Not anybody like Siv, because she is unreasonable in her demands: Wanting, not wanting, wanting the impossible.

Eric is going to get married now, be head physician, be a father. She thinks that this is all wrong. Her exciting red ram with the sure hands is going to join the flock and eat grass with the cows. How can such things happen?

She wants him to stay with her, in the same town and in the same place and in the same way: to sleep by chance, to eat by chance and to come together with her when they both feel like it.

She wants it to be like that, because she is not through with him. He is to remain with her until one day *she* has had enough. Then she would find it quite natural that he understood, resigned and said goodbye and thank you. Then he could begin to search for a secure situation if there was anyone who still wanted him.

She is very selfish and she knows it. Every now and then she sees the whole thing so clearly that she is ashamed of herself. She has many faults, but she is painfully cynical and honest with herself as far as she can see.

She is aware of the fact that she is a devil.

She is also aware of the fact that she is unjust to Eric when she gets angry.

She does not really want him to come whining to her to beg for a favor, and then another favor. If he came one evening and knocked on her door, begging and unhappy, if he told her that he could not do without her and begged for a yes, then she would abruptly cease to love him. She would despise him.

This is how unreasonable a woman is.

But now he is gone and Siv is quiet both internally and externally.

Her sister nurses look at her questioningly, but do not ask about anything. She laughs unnaturally, is merry and lively. They must never think that she has been deserted. She is just indifferent.

She starts to write again and now feels that she *can* write. For a long time this takes up all her evenings.

It comforts her, distracts her, the fact that she can write just because she has been left alone. She feels that she is a genuine artist. This is the way things are, yes, this is the way things are. Every great artist's fate is misunderstood loneliness.

So now she knows that she really is an artist. One day she will be repaid, become famous and admired, but she will smile somewhat sadly to her public: If they only knew what she has had to pay to become a great author. She is aware of the fact that these thoughts are lies, deceptions and vanity. She knows it, but hides herself in deceptive fantasies.

But she is not completely unhappy—she is never that.

Perhaps it is because she is so strong that she always has to look for a strength which is greater than hers. She has to have this because she is a woman.

She tells some of her sister nurses that she writes. Tells them this with a secret, shy smile. They seem to be impressed, and she enjoys this and tells it to more. She flies all too quickly on the golden wings of fantasy. She does not say anything definitely, but she makes everyone believe that perhaps she already has had some books accepted by a publisher—yes, that perhaps she has been known for a long time under a pseudonym. She will naturally not reveal this pseudonym—for very good reasons.

She smiles reservedly and says, "I can't tell you because then it would no longer be a pseudonym, would it?"

Yes, it is a blessing to have an imagination which can help you out of difficulties.

She laughs viciously and mockingly at herself. But we all love ourselves; therefore it is easy to take.

One day she gets a letter from home, from her father and mother in the yellow house.

She gets two or three letters a month, and Siv dutifully answers them. She tells generally about her work at the hospital, about new clothes she has bought and that she is well and doing fine.

Whenever Siv sits down at the table to write home, she sits very still for a while, letting a good deal of her thoughts and personality disappear from her body. She becomes a good, friendly daughter and nothing else.

She sends the letter and knows that her mother will be made happy by such a letter, but that her father will be dissatisfied and curious.

"I saw Heinz on the street," her mother writes. "He didn't see me, and he looked pretty tired. Do you ever hear anything from him?"

Yes, Siv has heard from him and has written, too, but he has not visited her in Copenhagen. She had expected him to, but she had not looked forward to it, and he had understood.

He had written to Siv that he had been sick again and that he was not divorced.

Siv had written and told him about Lars and about Eric. He had not wanted to interfere.

Blessed, understanding Heinz.

Once she had a moment of weakness and wrote and told her father and mother that they had been wrong about Heinz. He was good and understanding and had never done anything to harm her.

She had received a stern, worried letter in return. "You are not really still thinking about that man, are you? Father and I (it is always her mother who writes) "Father and I know that man will never be able to make you happy. And even if you do not like to hear it, we think it was his fault that you changed. You changed when you got to know him. He has given you ideas which can lead to your undoing. And anyway, he is still married.

Siv had torn the letter savagely to pieces: Heinz, you are misjudged, if anybody is. Father and Mother? If they only knew. Do they really believe that she is living like a nun in Copenhagen?

Her father surely knows what is going on, but he does not mention it to her mother. He is satisfied with a skeptical "Hmm" when her mother reads her letters aloud.

She can see them in her mind when they get a letter from her. She is their only child, their daughter—their daughter, isn't she? A bleeding sorrow lies behind this word.

Her father no longer works on construction sites. His health is not good. Perhaps it is a result of his childhood nourishment, bread with grease and potatoes, which is responsible. Siv remembers one evening in her childhood when he had read aloud something by a famous Danish novelist. It went: "He was gray—as most children of the poor are."

He had tasted this sentence. He had captured it just as one captures something which has been a bitter truth for one's self. He had looked over his reading glasses where the bushy eyebrows stood like a stiff wreath and had repeated, "Gray—as most children of the poor are."

He had nodded with approval: This was a good writer. He knew his stuff thoroughly. Because her father had been poor, painfully, wretchedly poor. He had lifted his head and fought his way out of it, and his life is a song of praise to hard work and success. He is also conservative. His lips snarl at all the unions edging in on the crafts. He had held out grimly and stubbornly. He wanted to be his own master, he did not want to be told to do things, did not want to be tied to pay regulations. His helpers had always been well paid. They had been his good comrades, and if a settlement resulted in a profit, he had generously shared it. But he wanted to decide for himself. He would share fairly, but he wanted to do it himself.

Oh, there are so many things Siv loves about her father. She has felt cries of yes and amen inside her so often that she has put him up on a high pedestal. Her father is so righteous, and yet—and yet.

Her father is so wise—and yet? He is a Christian fanatic. She cannot understand this.

She has watched him sitting in the evening with the plans for a new project. He had calculated, estimated, appraised, decided his fee exactly and conscientiously for the good of everyone concerned.

Months later she had seen him sigh and groan because precisely this job had resulted in too much profit.

He could not let it go by. No, his God-fearing conscience would not let him bear it. He felt like a usurer, taking bills and calculating and speculating.

He walked around for a few days fighting with his conscience. Then he put on his best clothes and went to the builder. "Look here, I don't like the fact that we have been paid so much money. We haven't done enough work to justify this and it's a matter of several thousand crowns."

He wanted to pay it back because somewhere along the line there must have been a mistake made in calculations.

This all had to do with the restoration of an old mansion. The owner at first looked skeptically, then with surprise and then speechlessly at Sacho. "Do you—do you think— that you've been paid too much? I can assure you that I'm completely satisfied with the work."

Afterwards, he had probably shaken his head: Is that man mad? But he will never forget Sacho. He has a soft spot for Sacho. If he later heard of some work that was to be done, he recommended Sacho most warmly.

No one who has known Sacho can forget him.

But now her father is old. He has grown old early. He carves many amusing and beautiful statues out of wood. The best thing he makes is one showing a minister pulling the devil by the horns. These statues can be interpreted in several ways. They are naïve and sarcastic at the same time.

They are difficult for him, because his hands are crooked and stiff. He breathes heavily. "What a mess!" He examines it and continues.

He has sent Siv a guest book. The cover is carved wood. It represents an old couple sitting outside their house looking at the sunset. And beneath is carved: "Just for an evening, just for an evening do I live here."

Does her father want to die? Siv cannot think so. On the other hand, there is something which she almost does not dare to admit to herself, but which sits in her brain like an evil certainty: Father is afraid to die, just as afraid as he was that time when Siv was a little girl and sat beside his bed.

One day she gets a postcard from her mother. Siv sees it when she comes home from work in the afternoon. She turns it over with surprise—from Mother? And only a postcard? It is not like her mother, who loves to write and talk so much.

She has written to say that Siv's father is very sick and wonders if Siv can take off for a few days and come home?

Of course, she can. She walks immediately to the hospital, visits the head nurse and gets permission.

They all look at her with gentle eyes as if they feel so sorry, so very sorry for her. But she hurries off. It is a big mistake for them to feel sorry for her because her father is dying. Everyone has to do that, and Siv cannot stand this hypocritical sorrow over death. Who knows whether it isn't a joy to die? And when the survivors mourn, it is for their own sakes that they do so. The dead one does not mourn. She steps into a telephone booth and calls home: "Hello, Mother, this is Siv. I'll be home tomorrow."

She finds out that her father is very ill, indeed. Her mother's voice is tearful, so tearful that Siv walks very slowly to the ticket office and orders her ticket.

She is going to go home to comfort her mother; will that be difficult?

It is a natural thing that her mother is upset. She loves her husband, and they have lived together for many years.

But what will her mother do after her father dies? The following day Siv sits on the train which is taking her home and ponders this problem.

Does she think that Siv can take her back to Copenhagen?

I won't, Siv thinks, I won't do it even if I'm thought of as the vilest daughter in the world. I won't manage it. No, Eric, it was a good thing that I said no to you when you asked me to marry you. I have no heart. But she sits and wishes that she were different, that she were a calm and loving daughter who was just what a daughter should be. Her mother deserves it.

She has always been good to Siv, spoiled her beyond limits.

But to live together with her mother?

She remembers once when she was a child that she had decided to be very pious. She would learn the Bible by heart, or at any rate, she would read it devoutly.

She had taken it up to her room one evening when she went to bed. A little while later her mother came up the stairs. Siv hurriedly laid something over the book. She was embarrassed.

But her mother saw that she had been reading something. She had come right into the room and had looked questioningly at her. "You are not allowed to read, Siv. You're supposed to go to sleep—and *what* is it you're reading?"

Siv did not answer.

Her mother had asked her a second time, crossly, nervously, "What are you reading, Siv?" She had walked right over to her bed and pulled the Bible out from under the blankets. "But, Siv, dear, is it the *Bible?* Why on earth would you want to hide it from me? There's nothing wrong with that. You can't imagine how much this pleases your father and me!"

Siv's piety was blown away as if it had never existed. She had handed the Bible to her mother and snapped, "Well, take it, then! I don't want to read any more of it, then."

That is the way things had always been between mother and daughter in the yellow house.

Siv sits on the train giving herself a good scolding. Your mother is old now, Siv, and your father is going to die. Remember, your mother is old and everything you find painful and tiresome in her nature has increased a degree. But it has increased so much that you can consider her a child, because you are the grown-up now, don't you think?

Pat her when you think she would like it, kiss her when you know it would make her happy. Tell her just enough about nothing so that she will believe that she knows everything. Do that, Siv, for your own sake. If you cannot bring yourself to do it for your mother's sake, you can do it for your own, you selfish creature.

Yes, now things are all right. That is the way it will have to be. Siv deserts her mother in her thoughts and begins to think of her father.

But she gets nowhere with these thoughts. She stands still. Nothing but a series of questions pops up which she cannot answer in spite of the fact that she thinks she has become so wise. You cannot put your father behind glass in a frame and look at him and say: "This is what he is."

He is just a question, a tragic, unanswered question. She wonders if that is what he thinks himself to be.

She walks slowly up toward the yellow house, feeling as if she had just left it the day before. She walks up the driveway and into the courtyard. There are no longer lumber and scaffolding to be seen, and the gravel has been smoothly and neatly raked.

Siv feels sobs rising within her. She grinds her teeth together. This is no time to get sentimental. She wipes her hands over her eyes. She must not go to her mother with shiny eyes.

She opens the kitchen door. Her mother is standing in the front window and has seen her, and she comes quickly into the kitchen.

She has also grown old, this little, round mother. It is not at all difficult to kiss her. As a matter of fact, it is good. Siv has become taller than her mother, or perhaps she stands more erectly. She pats her mother on her cheek, smiles and kisses her. This old wife cannot be embarrassing or cause problems. How on earth could she have had such bitter thoughts?

How is her father?

Ino looks imploringly at her: Siv *must* understand her. "He's very poorly." Siv nods seriously toward the door to the bedroom. "I'll go in to him." But she has to hurry to turn her face away, because, in spite of how strange it sounds, she feels herself about to laugh. Her mother's face is so childish, so dramatically possessed, that she is about to smile. Yes, it is just like old times—everything. But smile *now?* That would be dreadful.

She opens the door to the bedroom and stands a few

steps inside the door. Her father looks like a gnome, a pointed, thin, leathery, shrunken gnome. There is almost nothing left other than mouth, eyes and nose, and all his bristly hair and whiskers, which have now turned gray.

She should have come home before. She should have visited them every vacation. She should have smiled, made them warm, and laughed, letting them understand that they had a daughter. Now, now it is obviously too late.

She turns halfway around and sees her mother's swimming, watery, adoring eyes, which look so worried and childish that Siv feels that she wants to put her to bed, wrap the blankets around her and assure her that she has just had a bad dream.

Her father is asleep, propped up by pillows, his head hanging. He breathes heavily and in gasps. Her mother walks over to him and gently shakes him.

"Father, Siv has come home."

There is such a loving tone in her voice that Siv again has shiny eyes. My Lord—yes, just think, she has come home. It's just great, isn't it? Just think, Her Majesty, Siv Esruth, has finally let her light feet trip in through the door of the home of her old parents! She fights wildly with her tears. It will be impossible to hold out afterwards if she shows signs of a bad conscience. Her mother would use it like a lollipop for the rest of her days and would tell everyone how her daughter had understood at last.

She regains control over herself, because her father has awakened.

He blinks his eyes and opens them wide. They are shiny and bright. They are big and sit deep inside his eyesockets. Her father's eyes have always been strong and bright, but now they are completely—strange.

He does not speak at once. Her mother walks over beside Siv and nudges her confidentially. "Your father has been asking about you for days."

Siv asks, with her lips almost closed, "Why didn't you write sooner?"

"Oh." Her mother shakes her head. She refuses to be reprimanded at such a time. "I thought—I thought—that perhaps it was the wrong thing to do and I didn't want to worry you for no reason."

Siv feels a warmth rush into her. You, little, tiresome, painful, naïve woman. You had so much motherly love that you did not want to make me worry—make *me* worry, did you say?

And you have walked around with this great worry all by yourself so that your daughter would not be worried. She, who is to be protected and spoiled just as she was in her childhood.

Little, lovable Mother. Perhaps you love only Father and me. We are your entire world, and you have poured all your love into us.

You cannot help it that you were born without broad vistas, that you only saw a tiny, little patch of sky, the patch above your head.

Her father moves. He looks at Siv, laughs.

This grimace with his false teeth cannot be called a smile; it is a grin.

She realizes that her father wants to hide his weakness.

"Have you come home to see me? That's nice of you." He makes his voice thin and gentle as if Siv were a little girl.

She nods and tries to laugh. "Well, it's none too soon, do you think?"

Her mother gently interrupts, with reproach, "No, it has been much too long, Siv."

She nods. "Yes, you're right."

Her father looks at her a little sarcastically. "Did you think I was going to die?"

Siv feels herself jump. "No—o."

Her mother just says, "Sacho!"

He quickly shifts character, and Siv notices that it is her mother who is boss now. They have decided in advance how they will act when she is home. But her mother has to remind her father of this.

Siv finds a chair and sits down beside the bed and makes her voice bright and happy. "Well, how do you feel?"

"I am old, and I am going to die."

He utters this calmly and wearily. He cannot be bothered with pretty commonplaces.

"Yes, Father, but if you are going to die, you're not sorry about that, are you?"

He mumbles something that Siv does not understand. He has difficulty with every word he tries to say. His false teeth clop up and down in his mouth, and he does not have the strength to keep them in place. The well-known letters still hang on the wall above the bed: "Behold, behold, I am coming soon!" Yes, it would have been more suitable if this great Christian prince had come and had taken her father mercifully by the hand.

It is cold outside. It is autumn. But her father's body is to be put into the ground. There is nothing to be done about it. He is to follow the same path as everyone else. And he knows it, and shrinks from it. But he does not *want* to shrink from it. He wants to die like a holy man who has established peace with his God, as an affirmation for other Christians.

Siv seems to be able to read his thoughts, his fear and his resistance, his sure faith in Christianity.

He must keep his belief, die in his belief, for otherwise everything is without meaning.

She begins to daydream while she sits there looking at her father. Yes, who can tell whether they are daydreams or glimpses of truth?

I believe, Father, that you will go to heaven, but it is not the sort of place you have imagined; it is much, much nicer. You will probably wander around at first, restlessly looking for the saints who are supposed to be there with their palm branches.

But you will discover very slowly that there is no battle here, dear, brave Father, no bad conscience, no inhumane thoughts. You will discover yourself, your own soul which you have tied and bound. You will undo the ropes and breathe with relief, laugh a little at yourself, shake your head at yourself.

You will forget your fear, dear Father. You will understand that God is everything that you have never dared to do, that heaven is a place where you just—*are*. And then I will ask you to bend your spirit down toward me so that you will be able to discover that the same heaven is inside us both.

She says, "Father, you will understand me after you die."

Sacho shakes his head.

She repeats, "I know it. You will understand me after you die."

He nods gently. He has to nod gently because he loves her. "Let's hope so, Siv, dear."

Siv looks quickly at her mother and discovers that she is standing there nodding. She even says, "I think I know what Siv means, Father."

Is it possible? Does her mother understand?

There are so many strange people here on this earth.

But Ino has always walked around with an adoring, unanswered question about Sacho inside her. This wife is made of clay. She is a human being. God bless her.

She was born as a child and she will die as a child, but she will not have any difficulties getting into heaven, because she is a child. Little, stupid, wise Mother.

Her father gets tired. He wants to sleep. Siv has to prepare him for the night. Naturally. She is a nurse, isn't she? And her mother needs to be relieved.

A nurse comes in once a day and straightens up, but Ino explains to Siv that she has to do everything herself in the evenings.

Siv nods willingly and pulls herself together. She intends to treat her father like an old patient.

She removes the blankets, takes his temperature and discovers that the skin on his neck is thin and black. He has to be washed, rubbed with alcohol and oil. Otherwise he will get bedsores. Using a cloth she washes the two relaxed balls that hang like two folds of skin without muscles. She thinks with determination: This is nothing but an old body, but inside, inside it is my father—whom I adored.

When she has finished, she turns out the light. Her father has already fallen asleep, is tired and feverishly hot. Siv looks at the double bed and is happy that she is not the one who will have to sleep beside him that night. How does her mother stand it? How can she sleep beside this dying person? Siv's bed has been made in her old room. She drinks a cup of coffee with her mother in the kitchen. There are fresh cakes and cookies and new shelf-paper in the cupboards. Her mother has fixed things up because she was coming. She finds the cookies dry and washes them down with her coffee. She looks tired. "I guess I'd better go to bed and get some sleep, but don't hesitate to call me if you need me."

"How long are you going to be home, Siv?"

"As long as I have to." She says this—and means it.

The days that follow:

Her father begins to jabber like a child. He is feverish and unreasonable. Ino shakes her head and looks beseechingly at Siv as if she were the Lord. When Siv is making up his bed, her father grabs her arm, looks at her with swimming eyes and says, "You've become so *smart,* Siv."

This "smart" has a peculiar tone in her father's mouth as if he had tasted a juicy steak.

Siv smiles a little and is a bit touched: Dear Father, old man, you mustn't get too jabberish, you mustn't betray too much. Not after you've been so brave.

But Sacho grabs her once more by the arm. "Other men think the same thing, don't they?"

She has to follow his train of thought. "Yes, they do."

On her mother's side of the bed, which is covered by a white crocheted bedspread during the day, are pamphlets and books—religious writings. The Bible lies there, too. Her father can no longer read, but he insists that they lie there.

His mind opens up like an old book with torn pages: Lust, passion, piety, stubbornness, gentleness, meekness and pride. The pages have loosened from the binding. One can no longer follow them. They are stuck back in the wrong places and are frustrating.

Siv sits by his bed, wishing: You've got to die, Father. I do not want to learn any more. She feels as if she has opened someone's private letter.

Ino does not understand this. She makes excuses and tries to explain. Every now and then she just opens her eyes and looks hopelessly at Siv.

And Siv hides her face and her smile from her mother's despairing face. Because her father is also dirty and tells strange, stammering stories for no other reason than that they are dirty.

A moment later he has no idea what he has said. He apologetically shakes his head from side to side. "I've been talking nonsense, haven't I?"

And her mother says with conviction, "Yes, you have, Sacho."

She can look so worried and despairing at Siv's father that she seems to be a single crying sorrow. But later in the evening, when she sits with Siv in the parlor, knitting and chatting, when Siv tells her small, amusing anecdotes from the hospital, which she colors to make more exciting, then her mother laughs freely and heartily. She laughs until tears stream down her cheeks. She forgets like a child, laughs like a child.

A week and a half pass before Sacho is unconscious.

Three days later and the end has come.

Relatives arrive to visit. Her mother's relatives and friends and acquaintances. And her mother is sincerely sad, but enjoys the atmosphere like a tragedy in the theater.

Siv feels nothing when the end comes.

She sits together with the others in the bedroom and just looks at her father lying there with closed eyes, gasping for breath.

Somebody slips out to make coffee. Somebody else whispers to a third that her husband is also weak.

Siv sits undisturbed and just stares at her father's face, stiff, empty and tired. She recognizes the final signs from her experience at the hospital, stands up and closes his eyes when they open.

A sobbing begins around her. She looks for her mother, but she has buried her head in someone else's lap.

She straightens up and sighs, "If you will all go out of the room, I'll prepare my father's body."

They leave, one by one. Her mother comes over and strokes her father's hand. Her face is trembling so that Siv has to pat her on her soft cheek.

And Ino does not ask for more at this point, because this is *genuine* sorrow.

Siv prepares her father, slowly, carefully.

No, this is not true. She does not prepare her father, but his body. There is a big difference, and it is this difference which makes it possible for one to tolerate the strangeness of death.

She thinks of the other dead bodies she has prepared, and she is happy that she has always been careful.

She feels relieved, because her father is comfortable now. She thinks she knows this. Oh, who is it who has convinced people that it is painful to die? It is not true. It has to be good. She looks at the relaxed muscles and the peaceful features: Things are fine now, aren't they, dear Father? Your old body was no longer of any use to you.

She raises her head and shivers a little.

But where are you now, dear Father Sacho?

CHAPTER ELEVEN

The spring wind rushes across the dark earth. It whispers in the blood, whispers in the brain: Life is pleased to request that people be joined together in love.

Are you able to stroll calmly through spring? That is because you have known it for many years, so many years that your slowly flowing blood is a shield against the enticing whispering.

But if you are young, you hear its voice as if it were a shriek, a commanding voice to be obeyed.

The spring wind rustles the town's signs, rushes warmly and softly around the thick buds of bushes, makes small, curly waves on the Sortedam lake, where ducks and swans swim around in picturesque confusion.

It whips strongly and invitingly about Siv's hair as she walks beside the lake, blowing it into her eyes. She lifts her head, blows her hair out of her eyes, raises her hand and captures it with her fingers.

She is off-duty and has taken a walk along the Langelinje, but otherwise does not really know what she is going to do with the day.

Yes, she does know—if only—the impossible would happen.

Everything that has had any importance for Siv has always happened in the spring.

She likes all the seasons of the year, even winter, when the snow lies white and beautiful in Nordsjælland's woods, so clean and untouched, and with a shivering stillness around the stiff, snow-laden, expectant trees.

And the autumn, when you can walk bent forward into the rain and storm and test your strength against the fury of the elements.

Summer is also good. Then you get brown and beautiful

and can walk down the streets and show what the Lord has given you.

But there is something special about spring, when the sap rises in the trees and cats howl at night, when around every corner is a dog following a scent, when the men driving trucks have alert, gleaming eyes, and stop with a smile if you are going to cross the street.

The spring, when everything happens that is worth happening.

She kicks the cap of a beer bottle on the sidewalk, pursues it a few hundred yards and then sends it out into the lake.

She remembers a nurse who lives here on Østerbro Street. Siv will see if she is home. That will at least be better than walking along here feeling so terribly sorry for herself.

Gerda is at home. She is bright and full of mirth, easy to get along with. She invites Siv in, explaining that she is off-duty and is expecting a visit from her brother.

She says "my brother" with a sweet, enthusiastic smile.

Siv thinks crossly that she probably won't be able to stand him: a big brother? Brothers, protecting, boasting brothers who permit anything, but want their own sisters to be small, white angels and look up to the masculine root of the tree.

Siv is in bad spirits and is quite unreasonably cross.

Lars has gone, Eric has gone. She is through with life. And now it is spring. Gerda laughs at her, laughs to her, amuses herself over her. "Shame on you, Siv!"

"No, I don't want to."

"Listen." Gerda is interrupted by the doorbell ringing. Siv hears her happy greeting and hears a man's voice laugh with her, a deep, pleasant voice.

What had Gerda said about him? Her brother is a lawyer. He is surely a thin, daisy-like man with white hands which crackle like all his documents.

Siv sits up in her chair.

A heavy, broad man enters the room. His face is large and fleshy, his chin square, and he seems so big and heavy that Siv thinks he fills the whole room.

He walks toward her and she stands up and stretches out her hand.

Gerda introduces, "Well, this is my brother—and this lady is Siv Esruth, a colleague."

This *lady?* She stands there with her hand lost in a big, broad hand and feels with painful certainty that she does not look like a lady. She has not brushed her hair since her walk on the Langelinje. She has on a pair of slacks and a faded sweater.

But she stands up straight. And it is all the same to her if this man likes her or doesn't like her.

She thinks he holds on to her hand for a long time. Is it really a long time or does she just think so? His hand is warm and dry, and so large that hers completely disappears.

He lets go and mumbles his name. She does not hear it, but that really does not matter.

He laughs a little, so strangely soft and deep as if he were embarrassed or wanted to be careful with all his strength.

Because he is strong. Siv sees this and has to change her notion of what lawyers look like: They can also look like this.

He sits down heavily in the chair next to hers and puts one of his hands into his pants pocket. Siv looks at his hand and the taut sinews around his wrist, and a strange thought flies through her head: "Did he put me in his pocket? He dragged me down there and hid me like a secret in his clenched hand, didn't he?"

Gerda has not noticed anything. She has not felt that the air has been charged with a powerful electricity. This is only her brother, not a strange, disturbing man.

He talks with Gerda, now and then turning and smiling at Siv.

It is as if he sits there the whole time with an inner understanding: Hmm. Like a doctor who is examining a nervous patient, like a father who is calming his daughter or like a man who knows and waits. A heavy, sensual calm shines from him, a safe, masculine knowledge about the correct erotic partnership.

Siv has never met him before. He cannot know her—can he?

His hair is thin and brown, and he has lines around his eyes that become deep creases whenever he laughs. How old can he be? Forty-five perhaps?

Gerda goes out to make more coffee.

Siv shifts her feet nervously: I hope she hurries up. She rebukes herself: You are mad, Siv, you are mad.

She would really like to have a cigarette, but does not dare, because he would then offer her a light. And his eyes would look at her over the match. She would not be able to hold the cigarette until it was lit.

He takes an apple out of the bowl on the table and nods at her. "Do you want one?"

"No, thanks. I never eat fruit."

"Hmm." He sits there with the apple between his hands, letting it roll back and forth, and rubs it bright and shiny.

She can see a hidden smile vibrating around his mouth.

He slowly puts the apple to his mouth, revealing a whole row of powerful front teeth, and takes a large, lingering, juicy bite.

He looks at Siv the whole time, munching and crunching in a completely uninhibited and bestial fashion. Never has an apple been eaten with such relish.

Her cheeks become a burning red. She had better get up now and go. She should not be sitting here letting herself be bitten into. It is shameful the way he eats.

But she remains seated.

He throws the stem into the ashtray. He has eaten the rest, core, seeds and all.

She asks with a sharp voice that misfires, "Why don't you eat the stem as well?"

He smiles. "It's too dry."

Gerda comes back in and Siv turns to her with relief. "More coffee. That's good."

Gerda looks at them for a moment. "What have you two been talking about?"

The man turns and looks up at her with a big smile that breaks out from all his grooves and wrinkles. "We've been eating apples."

"Was that so funny?"

"No—o."

"Well, you look as if it were."

After a while Gerda says, "Now you two have to disappear. I've got to change for work."

She looks closely at Siv. "You're so pale and quiet. You ought to get some sun."

"Yes, perhaps."

The door is shut. Siv stands there, lost, looking at it. She could ring and say that she had forgotten something, breaking the hidden connection with the man who stands there silently waiting.

He says simply, "Come on!"

A very normal expression of two words, but just the same it puts a weight on Siv's body that almost prevents her from moving her feet.

She turns slowly and walks in front of him down the stairs.

They stand on the sunlit street.

He tosses his head. "This way."

They go into a sidewalk café, a chair is held for Siv and a drink is placed in front of her.

"A cigarette?"

She nods.

He lights it for her, and she has to look into the calm eyes which are not triumphant, not teasing, but just shine with a sure knowledge of this woman, Siv.

He smiles. "Has the cat got your tongue?"

"No, no. I'm just tired. I've got a headache."

Then he laughs. "Oh, no, you don't. Drink up so you can have another drink."

"Okay. Thanks."

He has taken her hand, which lay nervously clenched on the tablecloth. He opens it, finger by finger, leans quickly over and bites her fingertips.

She winces, but does not pull her hand back. A warm wave of deliverance flows over her. Is he bad? Is he good?

She does not know. She just knows that he understands her.

He carefully puts her hand back on the tablecloth.

"Give me your address and I'll pick you up this evening."

Her address? Her hand nervously clenches again.

"Are you a bit afraid?"

His voice is teasing, but his eyes are serious, questioning.

She breathes deeply with a sigh. "Yes, I guess I am."

He asks, quietly and gently, "But no more than you should be?"

She will not answer him. No, she cannot answer such a question.

She hides her eyes.

"Answer me, girl."

With difficulty, she manages to get out, "You're probably right."

He smiles again, this time with his eyes as well. "Yes, of course I am. Write your address down here and then go out into the sun. I'll come by at seven o'clock."

"Go out into the sun," he had said, "go out into the sun."

There *is* no sun. There are no streets, no concrete, rational things in the whole world.

There is just one thing beating in Siv's brain, holding all her senses in check:

He'll come by at seven o'clock. Oh, God, I can't stand it. I'll go to pieces. Where will we go? To a restaurant? To the theater? To his place? No, not so soon, not so soon, not yet.

She is silly and overexcited. It must be the drinks she has had. This is not the first time a man has asked her out, is it?

Seven o'clock. Oh, God, what a wild and exciting gift life is.

She buys an armful of flowers, goes home and fills all her vases and opens all the windows.

She has to pull herself together. A warm bath might help, hmm?

Her clothes lie on the rug, Siv, in the bathtub. Her muscles and nerves relax in the warm water, and she can think again.

The whole thing is so strange.

What if she should tell it to somebody?

They would not believe it. They would simply shrug their shoulders: an overexcited imagination. Such things simply don't *happen*.

But it did happen. No words of explanation, just the fact that you meet each other—and know each other.

She will write about it some day. Tell the whole world that life can be like this. So real, so painfully true that you become afraid of your own longings.

Siv has put on a dark red dress and walks restlessly around in her little apartment, straightens the flowers, looks out of the window, sits down, and stands up again. The clock will soon strike seven.

Someone knocks on the door.

She breathes deeply, but cannot find her voice. It is impossible for her to say, "Come in!"

Louder knocking.

She goes to the door and opens it.

"Good evening, little girl."

He smiles gently and has to push her to come in.

The door closes behind him, and he turns and locks it.

"What are you doing? Aren't we going out?"

This is released like a hoarse cry from Siv. She has not said "Good evening," not said "Welcome."

"Yes—later."

He grabs her by her shoulders, turns her toward him and pushes her up against the locked door, holding her tightly with one hand while he unbuttons her dress with the other.

She protects herself with her hands. "No, no, not like this, not now!"

"Stand still, girl!"

No tender commonplaces, no asking for permission, no caresses, only these words said in a calm, muted voice, "Stand still, girl!"

Siv tears his hand away.

He looks at her, captures her eyes, puts his hands firmly on her shoulders and pushes her against the door.

Then he lets go of her with one hand and gives her a resounding box on the ear.

He does not say anything, just looks at her.

She closes her eyes, presses her head back against the door and waits.

They stand like this for a while. He does not touch her. He just stands there silently looking at her.

She cannot stand it any longer. She breaks down. "I—I—"

"Yes."

A good, understanding yes.

He puts his hands around her neck and undresses her, sliding her light undergarments away with his hand. He lifts her up and lays her on the bed.

Siv's nakedness is partially hidden by the approaching darkness, but she reaches down and pulls a blanket over her.

Her eyes are still closed, but she knows that he stands

there looking at her. This silence, this painful, brutal silence.

She stretches out her hand and opens it toward him.

He walks over to her and shoves the blanket away with the palm of his hand. "My girl, my lovely girl."

His voice is husky now and harder.

And he begins. He grabs her legs, putting them up on his shoulders, bends her up, with his face against hers.

He enters her hard and violently. He does not kiss her, he just looks, sees that she is naked, naked right down to the bottom of her slavish soul.

Siv is transported and her body sails in a burning sea of fire. He continues, continues. Quiet, hard, masterly, gently.

She screams and tries to push him away. "No more—oh, no more!"

But he continues, holding her tightly, and forces his silent rhythm into her senses.

A new scream reaches Siv's lips.

He quickly puts his hand over her mouth, and pushes her face against the pillow. "Be quiet, girl, you'd think that I was hurting you!"

In a while the rhythm becomes softer.

Siv trembles. Her face is free once more.

"Look at me, girl."

"No!"

"Look at me!"

And she encounters his glance which knows the woman lying under him, and she captures him in the bottom of her dark eyes.

He laughs quietly, puts his hands tightly against her buttocks and the gentle rhythm disappears in violent power.

Siv's nerves are stretched to their utmost limits.

She drowns in a thick, black darkness.

Laughter, a loud, good-natured, warm laughter comes from this man who, a minute before, had been the devil himself.

"You fainted, you know?"

He has put her head in his arms and strokes her hair. "Are you all right?"

She grabs his hand, puts his warm palm to her mouth and kisses it, again and again. She puts her cheek against it and hides her face in it. "Thank you. Oh, thank you!"

She turns toward him, grinding her face into his body. "Thank you. Oh, thank you!"

Her voice trembles with pleasure.

She throws herself on her back, stretches her arms over her head and laughs up at the ceiling. How perfect, how good it had been!

Suddenly she is struck by the thought: I don't know his name, do I?

And she says, slowly, with a suppressed joy in her voice, "What's your name?"

He laughs, grabs hold of her and rolls her around in his arm.

"My name is Martin—and you can call me by my first name if you like."

"No, thanks."

"Don't you want to?"

"No, I'd rather not."

She hides her face. "You are so much older than I."

He has become serious, strokes her hair. "Be careful that you don't ruin yourself one day or let others ruin you. You are so genuine that you're almost too good to be true."

"It's wonderful being ruined."

"Yes, but it's not wonderful to be ruined."

Siv cannot be made to be serious now. "Well, to begin with, I'm dying of hunger.

He stands up and puts her on the floor.

You, reader, have you been offended?

If so, then you have forgotten how to love. You have forgotten the wild ride of love.

You have forgotten that all women are whores in the eyes of the Lord and slaves in their innermost femininity.

Siv and Martin meet each other once or twice after this evening.

But it is not the same. The magic has disappeared— and they stop seeing one another.

Something can be so true—so very true—that it can only be experienced once.

Almost an entire year on the New York Times bestseller list

TAI-PAN

95c
by James Clavell
author of KING RAT

Dirk Struan was the ruler, the TAI-PAN, of the
most powerful trading company in the Far East.
He was also pirate, opium smuggler, master manipu-
lator of men, and a mighty lover.

> "Packed with action . . . gaudy and flamboyant
> with blood and sin, treachery and conspiracy, sex
> and murder . . . grand entertainment."
> —*The New York Times*

- ■ A Literary Guild Selection in hardcover
- ■ Soon to be a major motion picture

*An explosive novel of how the U.S. Army
used its twelve worst criminals*

THE
DIRTY
DOZEN
E. M. Nathanson

★ *A Literary Guild Selection in hardcover*

★ *Now a major motion picture
  starring Lee Marvin, Ernest Borgnine,
  and Jimmy Brown*

The most original and savage novel of World
War II since *From Here to Eternity* . . .

"Tense action . . . gripping . . . highly recommended"
—*Book of the Month Club News*
"If you're in the mood for a marvelous thriller, read this one."
—*Cosmopolitan*

A DELL BOOK   95c

The Last Picture Show

by Larry McMurtry

explores the lusts of adolescent
innocence in the explosive
boredom of a dusty Texas town . . .

"funny and brutal at the same time . . . his
book has an understanding compassion . . ."
—New York Times

"Could easily be called 'Catcher in the
Texas Wry' "
—El Paso Times

75c

Don't Miss These
Bestsellers From Dell

THE FIXER Bernard Malamud 95c

TAI-PAN James Clavell 95c

THE LIE Alberto Moravia 95c

THE PLEASURE OF HIS COMPANY Paul B. Fay, Jr. 75c

LA CHAMADE Francois Sagan 75c

A DANDY IN ASPIC Derek Marlowe 75c

THE LAST PICTURE SHOW Larry McMurtry 75c

IN THE COMPANY OF EAGLES Ernest Gann 75c

THE PAPER DRAGON Evan Hunter 95c

THE EMBEZZLER Louis Auchincloss 75c

ODOR OF SANCTITY Frank Yerby 95c

CANNIBALS AND CHRISTIANS Norman Mailer $1.25

If you cannot obtain copies of these titles at your local bookseller's just send the price (plus 10c per copy for handling and postage) to Dell Books, Box 2291, Grand Central Post Office, New York, N.Y. 10017. No postage or handling charge is required on any order of five or more books.